"How about wa

Ben murmured, his lips pressed to the hollow of her throat.

Kate laughed huskily, shifting her weight so her body covered his. "How about now?"

"Impatient, aren't you?" Ben's hands cupped her breasts. "I like that in a woman."

"You'd better." Kate gasped as his thumbs and forefingers closed over her breasts, kneading them gently. "June . . . would be fine. Anytime . . ."

Ben smiled, enjoying her response. Then Kate arched her back, driving their hips together.

"The sooner, the better," Ben growled. "I'll have my lawyer draw up the papers."

"What papers?" Kate drew away from him.

"Just a standard prenuptial agreement," Ben said. "A prenup is a form of insurance, nothing more."

"I don't want insurance," Kate said angrily. "I want a man who believes in love. My love."

Laurien Berenson believes that the best romances have a strong element of fantasy and has long wanted to write a modern day fairy tale. *The Sweetheart Deal* is that book. She set the story in New York, a city she knows well. Although New York is not necessarily the most romantic of cities, it is a place where incredible things happen. Laurien saw her hero making his fortune there, and her heroine struggling to survive there while meeting her own high standards. And when they come together, the magic begins.

Books by Laurien Berenson

HARLEQUIN TEMPTATION
255–LUCKY IN LOVE
310–TALISMAN

The Sweetheart Deal
LAURIEN BERENSON

Harlequin Books

TORONTO • NEW YORK • LONDON
AMSTERDAM • PARIS • SYDNEY • HAMBURG
STOCKHOLM • ATHENS • TOKYO • MILAN

For Nancy Chiero,
who understands the meaning of friendship
better than anyone I know

Published October 1991

ISBN 0-373-25468-7

THE SWEETHEART DEAL

1

BENJAMIN WEST stabbed the elevator button marked L for lobby, then waited impatiently as the doors slid shut and the car began its silent descent. In its mirrored walls, he saw his own face, its strong features arranged in a pugnacious scowl. Looking away, Ben bent down and balanced his briefcase on the floor between his legs, then knotted the burgundy scarf at his throat, and pulled his navy cashmere topcoat closed over it.

Problems and solutions, he thought irritably as the elevator doors slid open, depositing him at street level. Some days there were far too many of the first and not nearly enough of the second.

On days like this, he wondered why he ever had gone into real-estate development. Construction at his newest venture, Westcon Tower, was already weeks behind schedule, and now building-trade workers throughout the city of New York were threatening to strike. The deal for a piece of property he wanted on the Lower West Side—which only this morning had looked like a sure thing—this evening appeared likely to fall through.

And if that wasn't enough, his driver had just called him from Kennedy airport to tell him that it would be hours before he'd be back in Manhattan and at Ben's disposal—thanks to the combination of road construction and traffic tie-ups on the expressway. Business as usual in the Big Apple.

If there was any more trouble tonight, it was up to Donald, his assistant, to take care of it. He'd left word where he'd be, but with any luck, Donald wouldn't need him until morning. After a day like today, Ben needed the peace and solitude of his country house in Wilton more than ever.

"Good night, Mr. West."

Ben nodded at the uniformed doorman who held the chrome-and-glass door open as he stepped out into the night. Though it was March, it still felt like winter. A frigid gust of wind funneled between the adjacent skyscrapers, stinging his cheeks. Ben paused to pull on his gloves and flip up the collar of his coat.

Behind him, the doorman scanned the street, looking for the long, black Lincoln limousine that normally would have been waiting at the curb. Tonight it was nowhere in sight. Perhaps he should have offered to call a cab. Then again, maybe not. From what he'd heard, his boss was just as apt to take the subway as ride in that chauffeured car of his. With a man like that, it was hard to tell what he wanted. And that face of his didn't give anything away, either.

The building grapevine said that West launched deals involving millions of dollars with the same nonchalance that most men decided what to have for lunch. Ice in his veins, that's what he had. Probably didn't even feel the cold.

The doorman watched as West turned the corner and disappeared, then he stepped back into the protective alcove of the entrance. When West wanted his help, he'd ask for it. Until that time, better just to leave things alone. A man like that wouldn't find hailing a cab any problem at all.

SHE SAW HIM standing in the glow of a streetlamp, his hand raised in summons. His dark eyes seemed fixed unswervingly on hers, though surely, thought Kate, there was no way he could actually see her in the cab's darkened interior.

Business had been sluggish all night. For the past few blocks, she'd been debating switching on her Off Duty light, turning in her cab at the garage and heading home to catch up on some much-needed sleep. Working two full-time jobs—as she'd been doing since January—was taking its inevitable toll. Eight hours selling dresses in an upscale, Upper East Side boutique, followed by another eight as a hack, wasn't easy; but if she could stick it out until September, she'd have enough money for tuition for her third year at NYU's law school. A goal well worth working for. She'd manage somehow. She always had before.

Now, as she peered through the grimy windshield, there was no mistaking the man's intent. He wanted her cab, and he meant to have it. With a sigh, she eased the yellow taxi over to the curb beside him. One last fare, then she'd head in.

"Where to?" she asked, shivering as a blast of frigid night air entered the cab with him. Automatically she glanced up into the rearview mirror to check him out. A woman cabbie—alone on the streets at night—couldn't be too careful. What she saw, however, was reassuring.

Though now tousled by the wind, his dark brown hair had once been carefully and expensively styled. From its soft sheen, she guessed the coat was cashmere, and the attaché case he laid on the seat beside him was fashioned of elegant calfskin and sported the initials BDW etched in gold below the handle. Definitely the sort of man to whom the contents of her cashbox would look like spare change.

Her eyes traveled back to his face, cataloging features that were vaguely familiar: a strong jaw, a finely chiseled nose, and brown eyes emphasized by thick brows and long, dark lashes. Then, as she put the whole picture together, recognition dawned. Her gaze flicked back to the initials on the case to confirm her guess. It was him all right.

For a split second, her eyes grew wide, then she quickly recovered. He liked that, Ben thought, observing her reaction. In his experience, women were more apt to make a fuss. Some smiled coyly and slid unobtrusively closer; others pulled out a prospectus, eager to talk money. Ever since *Cosmopolitan* magazine had named him Bachelor of the Month at the same time *Business Week* had put his face on their cover, he hadn't had a moment's peace.

The magazines' recognition was, he reflected sourly, a dubious distinction he could easily have done without. Now, however, this cabbie—Kate Hallaby, he read on the hack's license posted on the dashboard—made a refreshing change.

"Where to?" she asked. Though she didn't turn around, her eyes met his in the mirror.

They were blue, he saw. Large and luminous and, he realized with a start, cool as she gazed at him.

Her face was pretty, he decided, yet not the kind that would have stopped him on the street for a second look. A lightly freckled nose and full lips gave her a youthful appearance.

Glancing away from the mirror, he found himself staring at the back of her head and noticed that most of her hair had been tucked away beneath a battered

Yankees baseball cap. What there was to be seen was a rich, multihued chestnut color.

As New York cabbies went, he'd certainly seen worse. If she could drive as well as she looked, they'd be all set. "Is this cab available for out-of-town trips?"

Kate's heart sank as visions of a warm bed and a cup of hot cocoa receded into the mist. Nor was there any use in trying to dodge the issue. A sign posted on the back of the partition between them clearly informed him of his rights.

"Yes, it is," she answered reluctantly. "Subject to the rules and regulations you read there. The meter must be on at all times, and at the end of the trip, I'll need to collect double the amount shown. Also, you have to pay for all tolls."

"Fine." Ben nodded. "I'd like you to take me to Wilton, Connecticut. Do you know where that is?'

Kate started to turn and face him, then quickly checked the impulse. Wilton, Connecticut? Even at this time of night, that would be at least a three-hour round trip. But had he stopped to inquire whether that was convenient? Of course not. Obviously, as far as he was concerned, she had no more rights than the flunkies he undoubtedly hired to cater to his every whim.

"Yes, sir!" Kate snapped, and watched his brow furrow in annoyance. She shifted the cab into gear, glanced back over her shoulder to check that the lane was empty, then pulled out into the traffic.

Of all the passengers to pick up, why him? Kate fumed silently as she sped north on Madison Avenue. And why did he have to be going all the way out to Connecticut? He'd never know just how tempted she'd been to dump him back on the sidewalk and tell him to find his own way there.

But if she'd done that, her boss, Arnie—the dispatcher and owner of the small cab company—would have killed her with his bare hands. He'd made that much clear when she'd called in her fare just minutes before.

Speeding up to run a yellow light, Kate swerved to avoid another cab making an illegal turn, and swore liberally. The words that came from the back seat as the taxi rocked wildly, then settled back on all four wheels, equaled hers. Kate permitted herself a small smile as she glanced in the rearview mirror and saw that West had his briefcase spread open across his lap and was trying to work.

A workaholic. That's how the financial pages described him. The scandal sheets said something else entirely. But one thing was certain. Virtually everything Benjamin West did was good copy. Ever since he'd captured the public's attention by pulling off some of the biggest real-estate coups in New York history, his face had been plastered on every front page and magazine cover in the Big Apple.

The man wielded a lot of power—too much for his own good, or anyone else's. Kate gunned the motor as the cab skidded around the turn from 96th Street up onto the FDR Drive.

Damn! Ben grabbed his papers for the second time in as many minutes. If she wasn't hitting every pothole between here and the Bronx, she was coming close. What was the matter with her, anyway?

Sitting up, he leaned his head through the partition. "Let me guess. You forgot to mention that you'd entered a contest. First cab to leave its suspension behind on the street wins, right?"

"Sorry," Kate said sweetly. Downshifting, she shot into the passing lane, narrowly avoiding an oncoming truck. "I guess the ride is a little rougher than you're used to."

Ben gathered up his papers and shoved them back in the briefcase. "Don't worry," he muttered. "Compared to the day I've had, it's a breeze."

"Let me guess." Kate's eyes glittered as she echoed his earlier words. "You entered a contest to see who could evict more widows and orphans so that their rent-controlled apartments could be converted into Yuppie condominiums and you lost, right?"

What the hell was that supposed to mean? Ben wondered. Granted, he had converted several buildings lately. But he'd always filed noneviction plans with the City, and made every attempt to find alternate housing for those elderly or handicapped tenants who chose to move out. So what was she so hostile about?

The car slowed and Ben looked up to see that they were approaching the toll booth on the Triborough Bridge. Without saying a word, Kate extended her hand through the partition for the money.

"You know," Ben felt obliged to point out, "if you'd gone up to the Willis Avenue bridge instead, we'd have saved having to pay a toll."

"You're right," Kate agreed. Stopping only long enough to hand over the coins, she floored the gas pedal and the car zoomed away once more. "But then I'm sure you can afford it."

That did it, thought Ben. He wasn't accustomed to having anyone talk back to him that way, much less a smart-aleck cabdriver who clearly knew nothing more about him than what the media had chosen to focus on.

"Now, listen here." Sliding the partition farther open, Ben poked his head and shoulders through. "Just where do you get off, telling me how to spend my money?"

"You're the one who wanted to ride to Connecticut in a New York cab," Kate pointed out. "That's your extravagance, not mine. Then again—" she glanced at him out of the corner of her eye "—if the opulence of Westcon Plaza is anything to go by, extravagance must be your middle name."

Ben seethed with anger. She was goading him on purpose. She had to be. Powerful men, from politicians to chairmen of the board, had been known to quail at the thought of incurring his rage. Yet she seemed perfectly oblivious to the consequences. Kate Hallaby was as cool as a glacier. Along with everything else, that bothered the hell out of him.

Nor did it help that in order to talk to her, he had to perch awkwardly on the edge of his seat like a schoolboy in the principal's office. His position behind her placed him at a distinct disadvantage. It wasn't a feeling he liked, nor was it one he was used to.

"There's a big difference between spending enough to make sure that something's done right, and overspending."

"I'm sure there is," Kate replied calmly.

Prepared with arguments to support his case, Ben waited for her to comment further. To his annoyance, she seemed to have decided that the conversation was over. The ensuing silence only magnified his frustration.

Thick, wet snowflakes began to fall, and Kate flipped on the windshield wipers as she turned her attention back to the task of driving the car through the thinning traffic. Static sputtered from beneath the dashboard, and she reached down and turned off the radio that connected her with Arnie's garage. Once they'd crossed the bridge from Manhattan, they'd passed beyond its limited range.

Now, it really was just the two of them.

Taking a tighter hold of the steering wheel as the snowfall grew heavier, Kate wondered if she was being a little hard on West. After all, it wasn't he himself that she resented. It was what he stood for.

He was a man who was in a position to direct other people's lives. From what she knew about him, he did so casually, without ever stopping to think about the scores of individuals affected by his decisions. She had run into such men before—on a smaller scale of course—when, five years ago and fresh out of college, she'd taken a job at a legal-aid office in the Bronx.

Kate had seen what kind of havoc their high-level maneuvering could play with the lives of the lower and middle classes—people who were too poor or too ignorant to defend themselves. They'd needed someone who would believe in their causes; they'd needed someone who would fight for them.

For Kate, the first part was easy. As to the second, she'd gone back to law school to learn how. Four long years of sandwiching classes between jobs, of scrimping on meals and doubling up with a friend to save on rent. And still, it hadn't been enough. If the money hadn't run out, she'd have graduated in June. Now, having added the sales job to hacking, she'd set next January as her goal. There were times, like tonight, when it seemed very far away.

"You don't like me, do you?"

The question interrupted her thoughts, and Kate looked around to find that West was still leaning forward through the partition. To her surprise, he was studying her closely.

"I don't know you, Mr. West. It's impossible for me to say whether I like you or not."

"You know my name, and I haven't given it to you. Offhand, I'd guess that must mean that you know other things about me, as well."

Kate shrugged. He had a point, and they both knew it.

"I suppose you must have read about that divorce case where I was named as correspondent—the one that the *National Investigator* took such delight in covering."

Kate didn't turn, but she was listening. She detected a note of weary resignation in his voice, as though this was a topic he had already covered too many times before.

"Unfortunately," Ben continued, "what that rag failed to mention was that it wasn't the wife I'd had a relationship with. It was the husband—and that was strictly business. The woman decided that his work was taking him away from her, and she gave my name for effect, to cause a sensation. Of course, it worked. She became an overnight celebrity. The scandal sheets left out a few pertinent facts and ended up giving everyone the impression that she and I were having an affair."

Kate had heard of the case. Who in New York with two ears hadn't? The gossip mongers had loved it, milking every juicy detail for all it was worth. But she wasn't about to give him the satisfaction of being right.

Instead she said disdainfully, "Interesting you should think I'd know about that. Is it because I'm a hack, Mr.

West, that you assume I buy my reading material at the supermarket?"

"Of course not," Ben answered quickly. Once again she'd managed to put him on the defensive, and he didn't like it one bit. "I only thought that—"

"I know," Kate supplied for him. "You only thought that a poor little woman like me wouldn't be capable of digesting the *Wall Street Journal*."

"That's not what I meant at all. Dammit, you're putting words in my mouth!"

"And you, Mr. West, are putting your foot there."

She'd intended to gloat, but her attention was forced back to the road when the cab hit an icy patch and skidded. Lifting her foot from the accelerator, she turned in the direction of the slide. Only seconds passed before they were back in the lane, but it was long enough to get her heart pounding and adrenaline racing through her veins.

Ben expelled a long breath, glancing back over his shoulder at an electrical pole they'd narrowly missed. "That was close."

"Too close," Kate muttered. They were less than halfway to their destination and road conditions were worsening all the time. Deliberately her foot eased up on the gas pedal, slowing their progress to what was—by New York City standards—a modest crawl. At this rate, they'd be lucky if they reached Wilton by midnight.

"You're all over the road," Ben observed as he watched her continuing struggle to control the car. "Doesn't this thing have snow tires?"

"'Fraid not." Kate didn't take her eyes from the lane in front of them. "Arnie runs a rather low-budget operation. Besides, according to him it doesn't snow in New York City. It wouldn't dare."

"In case you haven't noticed, we're no longer in the city."

Kate couldn't resist a scathing glare. Her look said plainly what her words did not: *And whose fault is that?*

"All right, I admit it. Maybe taking a cab out to Connecticut tonight wasn't one of my better ideas."

If that was an apology it was too little, too late. If West had only been that sensible an hour ago, she'd be safe and warm at home right now, rather than out here braving the elements like an idiot.

"Didn't you listen to any weather forecasts?" she asked crossly. "They'd have warned you that it was smarter to hop on a train."

"Who has time?" Ben countered with a sigh. Then his gaze nailed her. "What about you? Sitting in this car all day, you must have heard something about an impending blizzard."

"I might have," Kate allowed, "*if* I'd spent the day here. But I don't come on until six."

"Six?" Ben frowned. "Don't tell me you're one of those aspiring actresses who spend the day making endless rounds to auditions that never seem to pan out?"

"Hardly," Kate said dryly. "Though I can see why you might have guessed that, considering that you seem to think women are merely something decorative to be displayed on your arm when a warm body is needed."

"I never said anything like that!"

"You didn't have to. Your actions speak for you. I may not read the *National Investigator*, Mr. West, but I do read the *Daily News* and Liz Smith has a field day with you."

"Oh, for Pete's sake." Ben flopped back on the seat. Unexpectedly he realized that he was enjoying their verbal sparring match. It had been a long time since he'd tangled with a lady who could think on her feet as fast as this one. Not that she didn't still have a few things to learn.

"Hasn't anyone ever told you that when you're going a few rounds with someone, the first rule of thumb is not to call them by their last name?"

In spite of herself, Kate grinned at that. She liked a man who could take it, as well as dish it out. And Benjamin West was no slouch at either. "Is that what we're doing, Ben—fighting?"

He listened to her say his name and liked the way she was able to switch gears so easily. He liked the sound of it as it rolled off her tongue with a husky cadence. And even more, he liked the way she smiled.

"I think so," Ben replied. To his astonishment, he really wasn't sure. Then, as he watched Kate bite her lower lip in concentration as she maneuvered the cab deftly over the slippery road, the reason for his confusion became clear: "Either that, or flirting."

"Flirting?" Kate choked on an unexpected laugh. "No way!"

"Ouch." Ben settled back in his seat and absorbed a direct hit to the ego. "When you go for the score, you don't fool around."

Kate frowned at that. For the second time in as many moments, he'd caught her by surprise. She had no intention of liking Benjamin West, but she hadn't meant to be cruel.

"I'm sorry if that sounded insulting. It wasn't meant to be. I'm sure there are millions of women who'd be happy to flirt with you. It's just that I'm not one of them."

"Too bad."

Kate snorted softly under her breath. Whatever his game was, she wasn't buying. He was very good at manipulating people, she told herself as she dragged her eyes back to the road. In his business, he had to be. But that didn't mean that she had to fall for his act.

Deliberately she changed the subject. "We're nearly out of gas. I'm going to get off at the next exit and see if I can find an open station."

"Sure," Ben agreed. "Anything you say."

The snow was falling more heavily now and was accumulating on the road surface faster than the plows could clear it away. Driving carefully off the exit ramp, Kate saw that they were in luck; one self-service station was still open. Stopping beside the pump, she hopped out and filled the tank, then stuck her hand in the window for the money to cover the charge.

"Have you had dinner?" Ben asked when she slid back inside the warm car.

"Hours ago," Kate replied evasively. There was no reason he had to know how many meals she found herself skipping these days. "Surely you're not suggesting that we stop now?"

"Of course not. But I was just thinking that if you're as hungry as I am, we might pick up something to munch on at that Dunkin' Donuts over there. My treat."

"Last of the big-time spenders," Kate teased and was pleased by Ben's answering grin.

"Hey," he said, spreading his hands innocently, "if the idea of a nice, gooey jelly doughnut doesn't turn you on, that's not my problem."

Kate laughed. "Okay, since you asked me so nicely. One gooey jelly doughnut coming up."

She waited in the car, keeping the motor running and the heat on as he dashed inside to make the purchase. When he returned, somehow it seemed entirely natural that he would climb in beside her on the front seat. Just as it seemed entirely natural to share a laugh with him when they both reached for the bag at the same time and their hands collided in midair.

"Ladies first," Ben insisted.

"No, you go ahead. I want to get back on the highway. Then I'll eat mine."

Once they were again under way, she made short work of two jelly doughnuts, then washed them down with a French cruller.

"I like a lady who knows how to eat," Ben remarked as she licked her fingers lustily for the last crumbs.

"And I like a man who calls me a lady." Kate had meant for the words to sound glib, but instead they'd come out as anything but. He'd touched a nerve, she realized, for her to reveal that much.

She felt him watching her and turned to meet his gaze. His expression had softened—the hard edges were all smoothed away. The magnate was gone; only the man remained. And she was intrigued by the possibilities. For a brief moment, the look they shared was so compelling, that she couldn't turn her eyes away.

If she had, she might have seen the ice in time. As it was, they never even had a chance as the tires began to slide sideways and the car veered off the road.

2

"NOW LOOK WHAT you've done!"

"Me?" Ben roared incredulously. He looked out the side window of the cab into a bank of piled snow that was almost as high as the door handle. "You're the one who drove us into this ditch."

"I didn't *drive* us anywhere." Kate reached down quickly to turn off the ignition. "Believe me, this was all the car's idea."

"Claiming your innocence by blaming the car won't wash." Ben lifted the handle at his side and tried to push the door open, swearing at his lack of success.

"By reason of insanity, more likely," Kate muttered under her breath, remembering the intimate look they had shared. Now, gazing at Ben's flushed, angry face, she saw no trace of the tenderness that had been there only moments before. Had she only imagined it?

"Move over," Ben ordered. "I'm going to get out and see if things are as bad as they look."

"Don't be ridiculous." Kate glanced down at his soft, Italian-made loafers. Obviously they'd been designed for nothing more strenuous than pacing a thickly carpeted boardroom floor. "You'll ruin your shoes. Besides, I got us into this mess. I'll get us out."

Knowing he was about to argue, Kate pushed open her door and clambered out. Things were even worse than she'd feared. The two wheels on the passenger side were buried in a large drift. Even if they'd had the proper tools to dig them out—which they didn't—there was no guarantee that the tires—bald as they were—could give the cab the traction it needed to pull away.

Tramping through the deep, powdery snow, Kate walked around the back of the taxi and leaned on the trunk. The car didn't rock at all. No doubt about it, they were truly stuck.

She next scanned the roadside; there were woods in each direction for as far as she could see. Earlier, they'd passed lights and houses. Now, all was dark and empty on the desolate stretch of highway.

"How does it look?" Ben asked, preparing to join her.

"Bad. Don't even bother getting out. We're not going anywhere tonight."

"You're sure?"

"Positive." Kate reached past him to take the keys out of the ignition. "The tires are buried, and there's snow caked up under the rims, as well. Using our hands, which are the only tools we've got, it would take hours to dig them out. I'd say our best bet is to sit tight and wait for a plow to come by in the morning."

"I see." Ben grimaced. So much for the quiet, peaceful night he'd hoped to spend at his country home. He saw her walking away. "Now what are you doing?"

"Making sure the exhaust pipe is clear," Kate explained as she stooped down to scoop away handfuls of snow from the back of the cab. "We're going to have to run the engine every so often for heat. This way, we won't end up killing ourselves in the process."

"Very commendable."

Kate stood and dusted off her gloved hands. "I thought so."

"What about the trunk? Is there anything we can use in there?"

"I was going to check that next."

Ben thought longingly of his sleek black Lincoln that boasted everything from a tiny, well-stocked refrigerator to a TV. He surveyed the cab's shabby interior and shook his head. When she'd said earlier that they'd be roughing it, she hadn't known how right she was.

"Hey!" Kate called, and he heard the delight in her voice. "We're in luck!" She slammed the trunk shut and hurried back around to slide in beside him. "I found a blanket."

Ben regarded the tattered bit of olive-drab wool she held in her hands with dismay. It looked as though moths had been feasting on it for years. "Is that all?"

Kate's smile disappeared, her pleasure turning to irritation. The prospect of spending a night in the taxi in the middle of a raging blizzard didn't please her any more than it did him, but at least she was trying to make the best of it. "Actually," she said, "there was a spare tire and a set of jumper cables, too, but I didn't think you'd be interested in them."

Ben softened. It wasn't her fault that they were stranded in the middle of nowhere. Well, not entirely her fault.

"You're right,' he admitted, trying to make amends. "A blanket will be a big help."

Kate gave him a disgusted look. "Don't patronize me, hotshot. In case you haven't realized it yet, it's going to get pretty cold in this car before morning. If you're too fastidious to wrap yourself up in an old army blanket, that's your problem. It sure isn't mine."

Very deliberately she made a show of winding the blanket around her body and pulling it close. "There," she announced haughtily. "I feel better already. Warm as toast, in fact."

Ben watched her effort to appear comfortable as she snuggled into the scratchy wool, and kept his grin to himself. This was one lady who didn't take guff from anybody—including from him. For some reason, that pleased him.

"So," he said, reaching up onto the dash, "shall we split the last doughnut, or do you want to flip with me for it?"

Kate eyed the bag with hunger. The three doughnuts she'd consumed earlier had only whetted her appetite, and her stomach rumbled impatiently. "A gentleman would offer me the whole thing," she tried.

Ben's answer to that was a short, sharp laugh. "Then it's lucky for me that I don't qualify. We're both in this together, sweetheart, and it's every man for himself."

"Really?" Kate lifted a brow. "And here I thought 'Women and children first' was the appropriate phrase."

Ben fished in his pocket and came up with a dime. "Heads or tails?" he asked, flipping it up in the air. "Your call."

Kate eyed the coin speculatively as Ben snatched it out of the air and slapped it against the back of his hand. "Heads," she answered finally, then grinned when he lifted his palm and she saw she had won.

Taking the bag, she pulled out the last doughnut and held it up, studying it in the half-light like a jeweler examining a rare diamond.

"I don't suppose you'd go for best two out of three?"

"Not a chance."

"How about double or nothing?"

"Sorry, big spender—" Kate glanced at his empty hands "—but from where I sit, you haven't got the goods."

"Oh, I don't know." Ben reached once more inside his coat. "I may be short on doughnuts, but I've got plenty of dough."

She ought to have been insulted, Kate thought. But it was hard to be offended when what she really felt like doing was laughing at the silliness of his pun.

She nailed him with a level stare, like a gunslinger squaring off to protect his territory. "You aimin' to buy me out, mister?"

"Could be." Ben opened his wallet and began to thumb idly through its contents.

Despite her intention to remain unimpressed, Kate's eyes widened at the sight. Right from the start, she'd intended to split the doughnut with him—just as she'd been sure that, had the toss gone the other way, he'd have done the same. At least for the time being, they were on equal footing. Sharing was the only way that made any sense.

But now, staring at the bills he flipped through so casually, Kate felt a queasy sensation in the pit of her stomach. The man was carrying around enough money to pay her whole semester's tuition—money that it would take her months of night jobs and going without to earn. Surely he couldn't be serious about wanting to buy her out?

Damn her scruples, anyway! She'd never find out.

"Put your wallet away," she told him, her voice scarcely louder than a whisper.

"What?" Ben looked up, and was puzzled by the anger he read in her eyes.

"I said put it away. You don't need your money around here." Digging her thumbs into the soft pastry, she tore the jelly doughnut in half. "Here, take it."

"No. You won, fair and square. The whole thing belongs to you unless we can reach some other equitable solution."

"Oh, for Pete's sake." Kate jammed the doughnut into his hand. "Just take the damn thing, would you?"

"Uh . . . sure." Ben accepted the gift and ate it slowly, watching while Kate did the same.

"I know that spending the night parked by the side of the road probably doesn't rank very high on the list of things you'd like to be doing," he said when they both had finished. "But do you mind telling me what you're so angry about?"

"I don't know what you're talking about."

"Like hell you don't. A minute ago you nearly snapped my head off. If I hadn't accepted that doughnut when I did, you looked as though you were fully capable of ramming it down my throat."

"Don't be silly. I'd have done no such thing."

Ben was unsettled by the ease with which she continued to evade him. He was used to dealing with people who jumped when he snapped his fingers; people who respected his abilities and his position. So why was this—his gaze skimmed up and down over her blue jeans-clad figure—this *cabbie* giving him such a tough time?

"Look," he continued irritably, "I'm not any more pleased about this predicament than you are. But from where I sit, it looks as though we're going to be stuck here together for a long time. The least we can do is try and behave civilly toward one another."

"I'm being perfectly civil," Kate shot back. The fact that she was in the wrong, and knew it, only made her feel all the more defensive. "And I will continue to do so, as long as you keep your wallet in your pants where it belongs."

"So, that's what this is all about," Ben declared, relieved. "Tell me, should I take your dislike personally, or is it a general prejudice against anyone that happens to have some money?"

"I'd hardly call assets the size of yours *'some* money.'"

Ben shrugged. "The first million's the hard one. After that, they're all pretty much the same."

Incredulous, Kate gaped at him. "You see? That's precisely the problem. You have so much money that you're totally out of touch with the way normal people think and live. The first million's the hard one," she repeated, shaking her head. "Give me a break!"

"I'm sorry," Ben said quietly. "I didn't mean to offend you."

To Kate's shock, his apology sounded genuine. She was only telling him the truth, after all. So why did she suddenly feel like such a heel? She was right about this—wasn't she?

"Don't mention it." Kate grasped the blanket in her fists and drew it more tightly around her, whether for warmth or as a shield between them, she wasn't quite sure. "I guess I am a little touchy on the subject."

"Why is that?"

"For a man who can afford to pay to have other people do his thinking for him, you certainly ask a lot of questions."

"Why not?" Ben countered. "We've got plenty of time and not much else to do. At least," he added, glancing down at the small puffs of steam that formed with every word he spoke, "not unless you want to count slowly freezing our butts off."

Kate jumped at the opportunity to change the subject. "It is getting colder in here, isn't it?" Reaching down inside the hip pocket of her jeans, she pulled out the keys and fitted them into the ignition. "Luckily we've got plenty of gas. There's no reason we can't run the engine every so often to use the heater."

"That's one solution."

Kate swung around. "Have you got another?"

"I thought you might offer to let me share your blanket."

Ben smiled disarmingly and Kate's insides gave a queer little jump. A warning, she decided. That's what that was.

"I did offer. As I recall, you turned me down."

"Ask me again."

Ben's voice was low and husky. The last time he'd turned the full force of his charm in her direction, she'd driven them into a ditch. And that outcome was mild, compared to what might happen this time around.

"Why do I get the feeling you're making me an offer you think I can't refuse?"

"Perhaps because I am?"

Reaching out, Ben took the ends of the blanket from her unresisting fingers and slowly peeled it open. A shiver sped down Kate's spine. This was crazy! She was fully dressed—complete with down jacket and sturdy hiking boots—yet somehow Ben made the gesture seem so incredibly intimate that she felt as exposed as if she were wearing nothing at all.

"Slide over," Ben murmured, slipping into the warm cocoon beside her. "There's plenty of room for both of us, as long as you don't mind being cozy."

Cozy? That was hardly the word. Try cramped. Try crowded. Try combustible.

"See?" Ben slid an arm around her shoulders and pulled her close to his side. "I told you we'd fit just fine."

"So you did."

"One thing you have to say for these old Checker cabs—at least the seats are nice and comfy."

"But still not nearly as plush as the ones in your limo," Kate countered determinedly. No matter how warm she felt at the moment, there were still barriers between them. She just had to keep reminding herself what they were, that was all. "I imagine that Lincoln of yours would never have landed you in a spot like this."

"Probably not," Ben agreed. He leaned closer as if confiding a great secret. "It has snow tires."

About to defend herself, Kate looked up and saw that he was smiling in a way that took the sting from his words. Slowly her resolve seeped away. She didn't even want to think about what was taking its place.

"Then again," Ben continued, "in case you haven't realized it yet, I'm a man who thrives on adversity. I love the challenge of taking a seemingly impossible situation and turning it to my own advantage."

"Oh, really?" Kate chuckled softly. "Well, feel free. If you can find any advantage at all to being stuck in a cab by the side of the road on a snowy winter night, be my guest."

"I don't know, things don't really seem too bad." Ben shifted his weight and Kate found herself molded even more closely to him. "Come on, try and relax. We'll never be able to keep each other warm if you insist on sitting there stiff as a board."

She was relaxed! Too relaxed. And that was precisely the problem. She didn't want to lean against him for support; didn't want to smell the odor of the citrusy after-shave that clung to his skin; didn't want to feel so comfortable in his arms. But somehow, she couldn't seem to help any of it.

She'd been up at six that morning, spent eight hours on her feet at the boutique, and the intervening time fighting Manhattan's murderous traffic. Her tired body ached for relief. Ben was having an effect on her, but not the one he had in mind. Her eyelids drooped as he spoke the next words close to her ear.

"Much better . . ."

Men, Kate thought dreamily. They were so predictable.

"Now, then," Ben continued in the same soothing tone, "suppose you tell me how you developed this phobia you seem to have about rich men."

Kate's eyelids snapped open. Talk about being lulled into a false sense of security! She should have known that the man hadn't gotten as far as he had in the business world by leaving things well enough alone. Still, she was too drowsy, too warm, too comfortable, to resist his probing any longer.

"The O'Dwyer Building," said Kate. She felt Ben stiffen. "In the mid-seventies. Remember?"

"Yes." He breathed the single word, then waited for her to continue.

"It was an old residential building in Brooklyn. My grandmother lived there for fifty years, until the day it was torn down to make way for an office complex that would be more profitable. She was evicted." Kate sighed bitterly. "Tricked into signing papers she didn't understand by an agent acting for a developer whose only interest was the bottom line."

"West Development," Ben said quietly.

Kate nodded, picturing the name emblazoned on the signs that had been posted on the building before it was torn down. "My grandmother came to live with us. She had nowhere else to go. Everything that mattered to her—her neighbors, her way of life, her independence—was gone."

"I'm sorry."

"You should be. The system allowed for the exploitation of the poor, and you took advantage of the opportunity. It's hardly something to be proud of."

"The tenants weren't the only ones who were used," Ben pointed out grimly. He hadn't thought of that project in years, but the memory was still raw enough to make him livid. "If I could have changed things, I would have. But at that point, I had no control—"

"The building carried *your* name," Kate broke in. "No matter what your intentions were, that makes you the one responsible."

This time it was Ben who withdrew. Suddenly Kate felt chilled and unaccountably bereft. It wasn't a feeling she was accustomed to. Under the circumstances, it was the last thing she'd expected. Off balance, she fought back the only way she knew how.

"You're at the top of the heap, Ben, and you only have to see what you choose to look at. Believe me, the view from down below isn't nearly so pleasant."

How dare she make assumptions about his life? She knew nothing about what really had happened back then, and even less about him. Nor did he care to listen to her side. Rather, she was clearly determined to think the worst of him.

"Think what you will," Ben retorted coldly. "I don't need to justify myself to anybody."

"No, you don't."

Why was she even bothering? Ben lived by his own standards, just as she lived by hers. Obviously her opinion meant little—if anything—to him. And right now, she was too tired to press the point any further.

Leaning back against the seat, she closed her eyes. "Look, if you don't mind, could we fight about this some other time? I'm awfully tired, and the only thing I'd like to do right now is sleep."

As quickly as it had built, Ben's anger dissolved. She looked so fragile there beside him, her skin pale and luminous in the glow of the moonlight. Dark circles marred the translucent skin beneath her closed eyes.

What was she doing, pushing herself so hard? Though her quilted jacket gave the illusion of size, he knew from holding her next to him, how slender she really was beneath its bulk. Hardly more than skin and bones. Didn't she know how to take care of herself? Or wasn't there anyone in her life who cared enough to do it for her?

Only moments passed before her deep, even breathing indicated that she was asleep. Her head was tilted back against the seat. Her baseball cap had come loose, freeing waves of rich, chestnut-colored hair that tumbled down around her shoulders.

Ben yearned to run his fingers through it.

Then, almost before he knew what was happening, his hand reached up to caress her cheek lightly, his fingers cradling her jaw in their grasp. She moaned softly, but did not waken. Bolder now, Ben used the tip of one finger to trace the outline of her full lips.

Sleeping Beauty, he thought fancifully, then snorted softly when he realized that left him in the role of the prince. Heaven forbid.

Besides, he mused, there was a passivity about that fairy-tale princess that suited Kate Hallaby not at all. Wherever she'd learned how to fight, it was a lesson she'd absorbed thoroughly. At least as far as he was concerned, she certainly didn't pull any punches.

She didn't approve of him. She'd gone out of her way to make that perfectly clear. Nor was he entirely sure what he thought of her—a woman cabdriver, and a mouthy one at that. Their lives were polar opposites in almost every way. Indeed, if it weren't for an odd quirk of fate, they would never even have met. After tonight, they'd probably never see one another again.

They meant nothing to each other, Ben told himself firmly. They were merely two people who happened to be in the same spot at the same time. So, knowing all that, why was he so incredibly tempted to lower his lips to hers and steal a kiss?

Proximity, Ben decided with a nod. That was the answer.

Then, still asleep, Kate shifted beneath his hands, leaning her face into his shoulder and snuggling against him. Ben pulled her close. Tenderly, he took the folded edge of the blanket and tucked it beneath her chin.

"Mmm." Kate smiled sleepily, nestling closer still. "G'night, Barry."

Barry! Glowering, Ben snatched his hand away. None of his women had ever confused him with anyone else— The thought startled him. One of *his* women?

"I love you," Kate murmured in the same drowsy tone, and to his amazement, Ben felt a wave of tenderness wash through him. The artless declaration touched him on some hidden level—arousing emotions that had no business at all being aroused.

Come on, Ben chided himself. Get real. Not only was Kate asleep, but she didn't have the faintest idea who she was talking to.

But when her hand slid up his chest, fingers burrowing beneath his coat for warmth, Ben knew he'd had just about all he was going to take. She might be shocked, or angry, or even offended, but by the time he was through, she was going to know who it was that was holding her in his arms!

Tilting Kate's face upward, Ben lowered his lips to hers. For a moment, they hovered above hers. Then she smiled dreamily and he knew he was lost.

Her mouth was warm beneath his. Its heat reached out to him seductively. Ben had meant his touch to be brief, yet somehow he no longer had a choice. When he increased the pressure, Kate yielded to him, shaping her lips to his.

Ben felt a fleeting stab of guilt that quickly disappeared as she began to kiss him back. He was too far gone—intoxicated by her response. A jolt of pure pleasure pounded through his veins as the kiss deepened. Warmth met warmth and generated heat.

He'd known he would find passion in her—he'd seen it earlier in the fervor with which she'd matched him, barb for barb. What he hadn't known was how her strength would excite him, challenge him, in a way that the pale, placid beauties he'd known before never had.

Then she pulled away. Her eyelids fluttered open as she blinked once, then twice, trying to orient herself. "Ben?" she ventured softly, his name emerging on a husky breath.

"Right here, Kate."

Shaking her head slightly, Kate said, "I can see that." Indeed, since her body was wrapped around his, he was rather hard to miss. Ignoring his smile, she slowly disentangled herself. "What ... When ... Were we ...?"

"Were we what?"

"I don't know," Kate admitted, her mind hazy. "I guess I must have been dreaming."

"No," Ben responded quietly, sounding every bit as bemused as she. "I think I was the one who was dreaming."

"Hmm?"

"Never mind," Ben told her. She saw in the half-light that he was still smiling. "Go back to sleep."

"I can't," Kate protested, but her eyelids were already drooping. "I have to stay awake to turn the heat on and off. Otherwise, we'll freeze."

"Don't worry." Ben's hand came up to stroke her hair lightly, guiding her head back down onto his shoulder. Kate heard him only dimly as she fell back to sleep. "I'll take care of you."

3

"HEY, LADY! WAKE UP!"

With a groan, Kate struggled to pull herself awake, the few hours of sleep she'd gotten having done little to alleviate her fatigue. Dammit, why was someone pounding a jackhammer beside her bed? She slowly opened her eyes, only to be blinded by the glare of the early-morning sun glistening on a sea of white. What in the world...?

The pounding continued. Kate ignored it and concentrated on her surroundings. Her head wasn't resting on a pillow, but on the side window of her cab. Her neck ached from the crooked way she'd slept on it, and there was a heavy weight pressing across her legs. Wincing as she straightened, Kate looked down, then instantly recalled the events of the previous night.

Benjamin West was lying sprawled across the length of the seat, with his head and shoulders resting in her lap. The blanket that had covered them both slipped down to the floor at Kate's feet. Still, Ben didn't waken.

Why should he? Kate thought, feeling miffed. He looked perfectly comfortable. He'd slipped one hand beneath her legs and the other cradled his cheek as he snored softly. His dark hair was mussed, his tie askew. There was a faint shadow of stubble along his jaw.

The man looked gorgeous.

And what on earth was she going to do about that?

"Hey, lady! Did you hear me?"

Kate jumped as the pounding resumed behind her. Gingerly she swung her head around, then blinked to clear her vision. It didn't help. A florid face, surrounded by the hood of a fur-trimmed parka, was pressed up against the window. But for the glass between them, they might have touched noses. Then she saw the snowplow parked on the road behind him, its engine sending puffs of silver smoke into the frigid air. Things suddenly began to make sense.

"Do you want help or not?"

"Yes!" Kate cried. "Of course!"

She brought one hand up and rolled down the window, letting in a rush of cold. She heard a groan, then the weight across her legs was gone. Kate didn't even turn to look. She'd deal with Ben later. Now there were more pressing matters at hand.

"Can you pull me out?" she asked eagerly. "We've been stuck in this drift all night."

The snowplow driver leaned back, surveying the damage. "Governor closed the road at two. That's why nobody's been by before this. You gotta rope?"

"Maybe." Kate nudged the blanket aside and scrambled out of the cab. She hadn't looked back and hadn't said a word to Ben. What was there to say?

Even her grandmother—with her concern for etiquette—would have been stumped by a situation like this. If there was something incredibly awkward about spending the night in the arms of a man you'd just met, that was nothing compared to waking up beside him the next morning—especially when the night had been filled with dreams such as hers....

"Let me look in the trunk," Kate suggested. "I think I saw a rope last night."

Blessing the air that cooled her heated cheeks, she tramped around to the back of the cab. The snow was fine and powdery, and almost knee-deep. Even with a rope, pulling the car free wasn't going to be easy.

She flipped the latch on the trunk and quickly found what she was looking for—a twenty-foot length of sturdy eight-ply. "Here," she said, reaching deep inside the compartment to retrieve the tangled hemp. "Will this do?"

"It'll have to, won't it?" asked a voice behind her.

Slowly Kate straightened. As she suspected, the snowplow driver was standing by the door, and the cab was empty.

Who was she trying to kid? After last night, she'd recognize that voice anywhere.

"You're up," she said stupidly.

"You're quick," replied Ben. "I'll give you that."

She didn't even have to look to know he was grinning.

"Want some help?"

"It isn't necessary," Kate began.

"That's not what I asked."

"You'll ruin your shoes—"

Ben glanced down at the snow-caked loafers. "Too late to worry about that."

"Or catch pneumonia—"

He reached out and took the tangled rope from her hand. Quickly and efficiently he coiled it in loops over his arm. "Are you always this argumentative in the morning? Or is today a special case?"

Kate gave him a grumpy look. "Today's a special case."

That should shut him up and it did. He threw back his head and laughed.

"You've got a nerve, you know," she said, slamming the trunk. "How anyone can be cheerful with that little sleep is beyond me."

"It's a gift."

"I don't doubt it."

"Besides, I'm always cheerful."

"Sure," Kate countered sweetly. "And I'll bet you can get me a good deal on the Brooklyn Bridge, too."

"Actually..."

Kate was so irritated she could have slugged him. She might have, too, if the snowplow driver hadn't come tramping around to the back of the cab. "You folks want help or not?" he asked impatiently. "I haven't got all day."

While Ben secured the rope to the taxi's front fender, Kate guided the huge plow as the driver backed it into position. When the two vehicles were only a few feet apart, she waved him to stop, then helped Ben finish tying off the rope.

"You get behind the wheel and steer," he told her when that was done. "I'm going to push from behind. That plow may be big, but I suspect it's going to have trouble hauling us out of this drift."

"I agree. That's why you ought to steer while I push."

"Don't be ridiculous. I'm much stronger—"

"Yes, you are," Kate agreed calmly. "But those loafers of yours aren't going to give you any traction at all. And without gloves, your hands are going to freeze."

Ben gritted his teeth and gave her a look. Never in his life had he known a woman who loved to argue the way this one did. "I'll make do."

"But, Ben—"

He opened the door. The palm of his hand, firmly applied to the seat of Kate's pants, propelled her into the cab.

"Bully!" she snapped, but he was already gone.

Muttering under his breath, he made his way around to the back of the cab. He must have been out of his mind the night before. Either that or faint from lack of food. There was no other way to explain the fact that he'd found himself attracted to this stubborn, opinionated cabbie. Thank goodness they were never going to see each other again after today. If he had to deal with this kind of insubordination on a regular basis, he'd probably go mad.

"Ready?" called the snowplow driver.

"All set, back here," Ben returned.

Kate extended a hand out the open window, her thumb turned jauntily upward.

With a grinding of gears, the plow began to move slowly forward. The rope between the two vehicles tightened. For a long moment, the taxi shuddered in place as the snow continued to hold it firm. The tires spun in the soft powder, and Ben leaned down to brace his shoulder against the trunk, applying the full weight of his body.

Then the tires grabbed hold and the car lurched forward. It leaped several feet, then settled, slipping from side to side on the icy shoulder. Inside, Kate found she had all she could do to hold the steering wheel steady as the plow continued to pull until it had succeeded in towing the cab out into the lane it had just cleared.

Letting out a long breath, Kate turned off the ignition and glanced in the rearview mirror. For a moment, she didn't see Ben at all. Then she realized that the two dark spots of color moving in the air above the snow were feet, sticking up out of the deepest part of the drift.

Stifling a giggle, she threw open the door and scrambled to the rescue. As far as Kate could see, her passenger was stuck in the deep snow, but good.

"If you say I told you so, I'm going to kick you," Ben said ominously.

"I wouldn't dream of it." Kate edged closer. The cab had thrown him backward when it found its traction and jumped forward. He had landed fanny first in the snow and sunk. From the look of things, the more he'd tried to use his hands to push himself free, the deeper into the drift he'd sunk.

"Are you going to give me a hand or not?"

Kate smiled. "I'm considering it."

"Well, consider faster. It's cold as hell in here."

"Pity you're not dressed for the occasion."

Ben cocked a foot in her direction. "Don't forget. You've been warned."

Kate giggled and prudently stepped back. He didn't look like the type to act on his threat, but then again, you never knew. That thought made her laugh all the harder.

"Lord, are you a sight! I wish I had a camera."

"I wish I had my hands around your throat," Ben muttered.

"What?"

"Nothing," he said pleasantly. If she didn't do something soon, he was going to...what? Inspiration seized him as he grasped the only weapon at hand.

By the time Kate realized what he had in mind, it was too late. One minute she was laughing, the next, the world exploded in a puff of white powder as a snowball grazed the top of her head and disintegrated into a shower of cold, wet flakes.

"Nice shot." A glance in Ben's direction confirmed that he was readying to fire another.

"I can do better. Now would you like to reconsider helping me up?"

"Threats?" A swipe of Kate's arm cleaned the snow from her cheek. "My, how low we've sunk."

"And sinking lower all the time," Ben pointed out. "Now hurry up and get me out of here."

"Your wish is my command."

"I'll bet."

He should have been angry, Ben reflected as Kate extended a hand and hauled him to his feet. She'd certainly left him sitting in that drift for a good deal longer than necessary. There was snow down his neck and up inside his pants. No doubt the cashmere coat would never be the same—and all because she'd elected to have some fun at his expense.

Then again, he'd always considered anger to be an unprofitable emotion. No, he had a different credo: Don't Get Angry, Get Even.

"There," said Kate, fighting back a laugh at the picture Ben made. The cool corporate big shot she'd picked up the night before was gone. Frosty the Snowman had taken his place. Deliberately she held his hand in hers until she was sure he'd regained his footing in the slippery loafers. "Now you're all set."

"Not exactly."

The mischievous gleam in his eyes should have tipped her off. Instead she'd been looking at their joined hands, curious why—now that there was no longer a reason—he hadn't relinquished his hold. Then his other hand came up and she saw that it was filled with snow.

Kate tried to duck but he was too fast. His fingers slipped inside the collar of her parka, tipping it back as he dumped the snow down her neck.

She screamed as the ice made contact with her warm skin. "You . . . You . . . rat!"

Kate jumped back out of range and snatched up a handful of the white powder, balling it in her palms. That was his idea of gratitude? Well she was damned if she was going to let him get away with it.

Her first throw hit him square in the center of his chest—a satisfyingly large white circle on his lapel, attesting to the accuracy of her aim. Her second try brushed his shoulder. Laughing, Ben shot round after round in her direction until Kate was every bit as snow-covered as he.

She ought to be beating him easily, Kate thought as she dodged to evade yet another volley. She was the one who had gloves and boots. She was the one accustomed to making her own way through the elements. Yet, from the determined look on Ben's face, he simply wasn't about to give up. And that made two of them.

Kate gasped as she hit a patch of ice and her feet shot out from under her. She found herself sitting in the snow with Ben, a snowball clutched in each hand, triumphantly towering over her. "You wouldn't!" she giggled.

"I might."

"Fiend!"

"First a bully, then a rat," Ben remarked. "Now a fiend. Lucky for me, I don't thrive on approval."

With a loud sigh, Kate readied herself for the barrage. "Well, go ahead. If you're going to throw them, do it and get it over with."

He did, and the snowballs thudded harmlessly into the drifts on either side of her body. "Come on, Kate." Ben offered her a hand. "Up you go."

She took his hand and allowed herself to be pulled free. And why not? Moments earlier, she'd done the same for him. But in the intervening time, something had changed. Was it the competition of trying to best one another, or the shared laughter that had gone along with it?

All Kate knew was that even when she'd gotten to her feet, Ben didn't stop pulling. She found herself drawn into his arms. She braced her palms against his chest as his hands slid up her sides. Nestling close, they both took a moment to catch their breath.

Kate finally lifted her head and saw that Ben was watching her. Just watching quietly and waiting. There was an ease to the way he held her, as though standing knee-deep in snow by the side of the highway with a woman in his arms was the most natural thing in the world.

Only it didn't feel that way to Kate. Pinpricks raced across her skin. She told herself she was reacting to the cold, and maybe she was. But how did that explain the excitement—the feeling that she was poised on the brink of something wonderful?

Behind them, the snowplow suddenly leapt to life with a thunderous roar. Startled, Kate jumped back. She glanced around guiltily and saw that while they'd been occupied, the driver had untied and coiled the tow rope, laying it neatly on the hood of the cab.

"I'd forgotten all about him," she murmured.

"So did I." Ben lifted a hand as the plow lumbered off down the road, and the rear lights flashed in reply.

"We never even said thank-you." Kate gave her head a faint shake. "He probably thinks we're crazy."

"We probably are."

The bewilderment in his tone made her smile. She was perversely delighted that he seemed as confused as she was about what had happened between them. "Come on," she said, poking a finger in his ribs. "Admit it, the snowball fight was fun."

"Childish," Ben corrected firmly, then raised a hand to forestall the objection he knew was coming. "If you're about to call me another name, I'll pass."

"I wouldn't dream of it." About to do just that, Kate settled for clicking her tongue instead. "If you can't recognize a good time when it comes up and smacks you in the chest—" a flick of her gloved fingers cleaned the imprint of a snowball from the lapel of his coat "—that's not my problem."

Ben's eyebrow lifted. "Are you insinuating it's mine?"

"I wouldn't be the first to call you a workaholic."

"You won't be the last, either."

"Then you might consider taking it to heart." Kate reached around and brushed off the seat of her pants. "Studies say that people who play games live longer."

"So do Russian peasants who eat yogurt."

"Maybe." She considered that. "But they're not my concern at the moment."

"And I am?" With effort, Ben contained his amusement.

"You're my fare," Kate replied, as though that explained everything.

Ben threw up his hands. She could probably go on like this all day. The woman thrived on argument. It charged her batteries the way food fueled others. He shifted uncomfortably as cold water—the remains of the melting snow—began to trickle down into his underwear.

"All right," he said finally. "If it will make you happy, I'll admit it. It was fun. Now are you satisfied?"

Kate cocked her head to one side, hazarding a guess as to the source of his discomfort. "Not yet," she answered with a smile. "But I'm getting there."

IT ONLY TOOK A FEW minutes to get the cab back on the road. Kate warmed up the engine thoroughly and set the heater running full blast. In no time at all, both she and Ben were beginning to thaw and the smell of wet wool permeated the air.

Though it was almost seven and the first plow had been through, the parkway was still deserted. When Ben turned on the radio, they found out why. All schools and most businesses were closed for the day. Motorists were advised to remain home—except in case of emergency—because the road conditions were still treacherous.

"I can see why," said Kate, struggling with the skidding cab. Noting the expression on Ben's face, she added, "Don't look at me like that. I'm usually a very good driver."

"I'm sure you are," he replied calmly. "Nobody could handle this mess well without snow tires. It's a good thing we're almost there." Moments later, he directed her off the last New Canaan exit, where they traveled north, then east, and headed into back-country Wilton.

"You really do live out in the boonies, don't you?" she remarked as Ben pointed toward a narrow driveway that led off into a bank of trees.

"This is where I come when I want to get away from it all. I've learned from experience that if you make it easy for people to follow you, they will."

"There are always telephones."

"I turn them off."

"Fax machines."

Ben shot her a look. "Not at my house."

She grinned at his vehemence and concentrated on steering. Beyond the trees, the road widened and Kate lifted her gaze to take in the beauty of the setting. In the midst of the woods, a large meadow had been cleared. Covered with a deep blanket of new snow, it glistened in the morning light. Ice coated the low stone wall that bounded the open field and shimmered on the stark, leafless branches of the trees.

The entire scene sparkled like a winter wonderland. Kate sighed with appreciation, then noticed that Ben was watching her from across the seat.

"Winter doesn't look like this in the city," she said softly.

"Amazing, isn't it? After you get used to the dirty slush that passes for snow in New York, it's hard to remember that this is what it really looks like."

The house, a large red brick Georgian with high white columns that ran the length of the porch, stood off to one side. Though beautiful in its own right, it didn't dominate the panorama. The view held that distinction.

Their long drive was finally drawing to a close. The camaraderie that had developed between them during the trip was nice, but Kate didn't fool herself into believing that it was meant to last. In a minute, Ben would go his way and she'd go hers. That was how things were meant to be.

The taxi stopped and Ben got out. As he stepped around and opened the back door to retrieve his briefcase, Kate glanced automatically at the meter. Its numbers were still frozen at the point they'd reached the night before. With everything that had happened since, she'd forgotten to turn it back on that morning.

"Something wrong?" Ben asked, appearing beside her open window.

"No." Kate swallowed heavily, already accepting the loss.

Ben followed her gaze to the meter. "That can't be right."

"It's close enough."

"No, it's not." He straightened and pulled out his wallet, peeling off several large bills that he folded and held out to her.

"You must be kidding!" Kate gasped, trying not to stare at the amount.

"Why?"

"That's too much."

"I don't think so." Ben put the money in her palm and closed her fingers over it. "Don't forget, in our case you have to measure not only distance, but time. If the meter had been running all night, just think of the bill I'd have racked up."

"I am," said Kate, gaping at the money. "You just paid it."

"Good. That's settled. Put the money away." Ben watched as she did so, then opened Kate's door. "Now, come on inside. The least I can do is feed you a good breakfast before you go."

"I can't," Kate protested, even as she found herself being drawn to her feet.

"Why not?"

"I have to get back."

"This minute?" Clutching her hand, Ben started up the wide steps to his front door.

Of course, he really ought to let her go. Hadn't he been looking forward to doing just that all morning? But for some unexplainable reason, he found himself stalling. Good manners, Ben decided. That and common sense. Only an idiot would want to get back out on those roads in that excuse for a car.

"Yes," replied Kate. "This minute."

"I'm not going to argue with you on this."

"Fine," she answered. "Then don't."

She really did have to get back. For one thing, there was her job at the boutique. For another, if she was going to go, she wanted to do it quickly. She and Ben were passing acquaintances. That's all they were ever destined to be and she had no intention of pretending otherwise.

"But you must be hungry." As they reached the top of the steps, the door swung open before them. Ben's gaze shifted from Kate to the trim, balding, older man who awaited their entrance. "Good morning, Parker."

"Sir." The man nodded, glancing at Kate, then at the cab behind them. "If you don't mind going on in, I'll go call off the helicopter."

"What helicopter?" As Ben's attention shifted, Kate took the opportunity to remove her hand from his.

"Just a small search party. I did wonder where you were."

"I'm a grown man, Parker."

The houseman gave him a wounded look. "That doesn't change the fact that you were missing. For all I knew, you could have been belly-up in the river. I thought it best to find out."

"Quite right," Ben agreed, tongue in cheek. "Go on, then. We'll see to ourselves for the moment. When you're done, I'd like breakfast set out in the sunroom."

When he turned back to Kate, she was grinning. "A search party?" she inquired, arching a brow.

Ben shrugged. "Parker likes to overreact. He has a flare for the dramatic."

Kate glanced around the ornate, two-story foyer. "Looks to me like he's in the right place."

"Make fun if you want. At least it's warm and dry. Not to mention well stocked." His gaze slid downward. "Stomach feeling a little empty, is it?"

It was, thought Kate, but that wasn't any of his business. Helicopter search indeed! If she'd been looking for something to remind her of the differences between them, she could hardly have done better than that.

"Look," she said, backing away, "I appreciate the offer, but I really have to be going."

"If that's what you want..." Ben let the question hang in the air between them.

"It is."

"At least let me pack you a bag of muffins or fruit to eat while you drive."

Kate was surprised by the offer, and also tempted. In so many ways, Benjamin West was turning out to be not at all what she'd expected. For a moment, she thought it was her resolve that was weakening, then realized it was her knees.

The accumulated effect of too many missed meals and too little sleep was taking its toll. She turned back toward the doorway, gulping in a breath of cold air, hoping it would revive her. It was too late. The world dimmed to black.

"Ben?" Kate whispered. The word roared in her ears.

He turned to face her, and she saw his eyes widen.

"Would you catch me, please?"

His hands came up, and they were the last things Kate saw as she fainted into his arms.

4

FOR THE SECOND TIME in twelve hours, Kate awoke without a clue to where she was. The goose-down pillow beneath her head was unfamiliar, as was the soft blue comforter she had snuggled up next to her cheek. This time, however, reorienting herself took only a moment as she sat up and looked around the beautifully furnished room.

She'd fainted, Kate remembered with a sigh. And Ben had caught her. Now here she was, in what had to be one of the guest bedrooms upstairs in that enormous house.

It was amazing what an extra hour in a soft bed could accomplish, because she certainly did feel much better—and as hungry as a spring bear. But then that was easily fixed; she'd simply hop downstairs and take Ben up on his offer of breakfast, before heading back into the city to work.

But even as she resolved to do just that, Kate recognized that something was wrong. Her gaze shifted to the darkening shadows that ran the length of the room, then to the windows, which revealed the dusk of twilight outside. Concerned now, she searched for a clock and found one on the bedside table.

It was five-thirty.

With a small cry, Kate tossed back the covers and scrambled out of bed. Ben couldn't have let her sleep all day—could he? She crossed the room to the nearest window, only to have her fears confirmed. From this vantage point, looking westward out over the snow-covered lawn, she could see the sun setting over a copse of trees.

Whirling away from the window, Kate muttered furiously under her breath. A rose-colored chintz chair in the corner held the rest of her clothes: the baseball cap balanced on its arm, her sweater and down jacket piled on the seat, her boots neatly lined up underneath. Quickly she grabbed the pullover and shoved her arms into the sleeves.

"Some people have to punch a time clock," she grumbled, her voice muffled as she pulled the sweater over her head. "But I guess that never occurred to him."

It had, however, occurred to the man who owned the boutique where she was employed. His rules were specific, and strictly enforced. If one of his saleswomen wasn't coming in to work, she needed two things: a damn good excuse, and the name of another employee who was going to take her place. Today, fast asleep, Kate had provided neither.

She picked up her boots and jammed her feet inside. Maybe Ben had thought he was doing her a favor by letting her rest, but that still didn't excuse his behavior. By taking the decision out of her hands, he had assumed too much—an act of arrogance that would cost her her job.

Cap and jacket in hand, Kate threw open the bedroom door and looked both ways to get her bearings. At one end of the hallway was a staircase. With a long stride and an angry scowl, she started toward it.

DOWN IN THE LIBRARY, Ben hung up the phone and leaned back. The supple leather desk chair tilted beneath him as he braced both elbows on its arms and built his fingers into a steeple.

Maybe it was time to go look in on Kate again, he mused. The fact that she had slept so long, and so deeply, only reinforced his belief that he had made the right decision in putting her to bed and leaving her there. The lady had worn herself to a frazzle, and if she didn't have enough sense to see that, then it was a good thing for her that he had.

When he'd begun his trip to the country the evening before, he'd never envisioned spending the entire day here. Still, things hadn't turned out badly. He'd been able to accomplish most of what he wanted over the phone. Everything else had simply been tabled until tomorrow.

People would wait if they had to. As far as business dealings went, he was worth it. They knew it, and so did he. In fact, Ben thought, his lips lifting in a reluctant smile, the only person who didn't treat him with a degree of respect that at times was almost laughable, was the smart-aleck female cabbie asleep upstairs.

Twice, so far, he'd been up to check on her. No, make that three times. He couldn't say just what exactly it was that had drawn him up the stairs each time. A concern for her welfare? Certainly. And a need to see that she was resting comfortably.

But he'd accomplished all that in his first visit, Ben admitted to himself, thinking back to the way he'd stood quietly in the doorway, his fingers resting on the glass knob. He'd meant to go inside the room, yet somehow he couldn't take the first step.

At the time, he'd told himself she deserved her privacy. But that wasn't what had held him back. No. The reason for that was something more: a reluctance that had everything to do with the memory of the last time he'd watched her sleep—the long night when he'd held her in his arms.

And so Ben had stood in the doorway; unable to go farther, unable to stay away. There'd been no sound from where she lay, nor any movement, either, save the gentle rise and fall of the quilt he'd pulled all the way up to her chin. He was glad to see she slept so peacefully, and was more than a little surprised that it mattered to him at all.

Yet there was something about Kate that aroused his instinct to protect and safeguard. Was it her fragile slenderness, so apparent when he'd carried her upstairs? Or was it the way she had of squaring off with him, jumping into the fray as if common sense and care for her own safety were the last things on her mind?

Ben just didn't know. As accustomed as he was to having all the answers, for the moment he was pleasantly baffled. For the time being, that was enough.

Ben righted his chair and stood. Three quick strides took him to the open door. He'd barely had time to turn the corner to the stairway when he saw Kate at the top, about to descend.

The dark shadows were gone from beneath her eyes. The long sleep had done her a world of good. It had also blurred some of the hard edges that she seemed to work so hard to maintain.

Kate's thick chestnut hair, hidden beneath the cap the night before, was now loose and tousled. Her clothes were rumpled, and her cheeks flushed a becoming shade of pink. The combination gave her a softness, a vulnerability that Ben hadn't seen before.

At least that's what he surmised until his gaze reached her eyes. Icy blue and hard as steel, they were trained on him as she paused on the top step. Whatever she was feeling, it wasn't gratitude. He leaned back against the doorjamb and prepared himself for a fight.

Dammit, thought Kate, staring down at him with chagrin. This was the man whose careless maneuvering had disrupted her life. She should be angry. No, she *was* angry. And yet the sight of Benjamin West waiting at the foot of the stairs gave her a small thrill.

I am not glad to see him, Kate told herself. She grasped the banister and started down the stairs. Well, maybe I am...just a little. But really, hardly at all. This last protest was one too many. By the time she reached the foot of the stairs, Kate was firmly on the offensive.

"How could you have let me sleep all day?" she demanded. "Look what time it is!"

Making a production of lifting his arm and checking his watch he announced, "Five forty-five," as though there were nothing wrong with that fact. "And good evening to you, too."

"Good? There's nothing good about it!"

Kate spun away. At the foot of the stairway, they'd been only inches apart. Ben's hand had brushed her arm as he lowered it to his side. They were too close, and she was entirely too aware of that.

She'd known men who shed their aura of competence as soon as they loosened their ties and took off their suits. Unfortunately, Ben wasn't among them. Even in his country clothes—jeans and a thick, cream-colored fisherman's-knit sweater—his power wasn't diminished in the slightest. If anything, he looked sexier and more masculine than ever.

Perfect, thought Kate. Just perfect. Exactly what she needed to thoroughly gum up the works.

"Is something wrong?"

"Something?" Kate met his gaze. "Everything is wrong. And that's only the beginning."

"Tell me about it."

His voice was warm and deep. Worse, he actually sounded as if he cared. Kate told herself it was probably his business voice, honed to perfection after years of practice.

"For starters, I've lost my job. And on top of that, Arnie must be frantic. For all he knows, his cab and I have both disappeared—"

Ben held up a hand for silence. To his surprise, he got it. "If that's what you're concerned about, don't be. I called Arnie this morning and explained what happened. Once I got through outlining the situation, he wasn't upset at all."

Kate's eyes narrowed. Arnie was always upset. It was his nature. And just what exactly did Ben mean by "outlining the situation"?

"He said to tell you that he wants you back," Ben continued. "But only when you're well fed and well rested."

"*Arnie* said that?"

"His exact words."

"I'll bet."

"Actually," Ben went on, ignoring her skepticism, "he was very understanding."

"This was after you told him who you were," she accused.

"Of course, I told him who I was. Why wouldn't I?"

"No reason," replied Kate, wishing she'd been there to hear the exchange. Arnie was a firm believer in the power of intimidation, running his garage with all the finesse of a marine boot camp. This was probably the first time in a long time that someone had succeeded in intimidating him. And for Benjamin West, it probably hadn't taken any effort. All he'd had to do was mention his name.

"At any rate, you haven't lost your job, so you needn't worry on that account."

As quickly as it had come, Kate's amusement vanished. "You don't understand. Hacking is only my night job. I work days at a boutique up on Madison. Or I guess I should say I *worked* at a boutique on Madison. Unless . . ." Her brow furrowed as a sudden thought struck her. "Was the snow bad in New York? It didn't shut down the city, did it?"

She looked so hopeful, Ben found he was sorry to have to disappoint her. "Not even close, I'm afraid. The worst of the storm hit Connecticut. New York only got a dusting."

"Oh, well." Kate's shoulders rose and fell in a resigned shrug. "So much for working for Mr. Raphael."

"Who?"

"The owner of the boutique," Kate explained, fielding Ben's stare. "And don't look at me like that. I didn't name him."

"I'll bet his mother didn't, either."

It was his smile that did it—wide, amused and hopelessly engaging. Kate found her mood lightening. "Actually, you're right. I got a look at some of his papers once. His real name is Melvin Schwartz."

"I think I prefer that to the alternative."

"Easy for you to say," Kate sniffed. "You're not trying to sell pricey designer dresses to Manhattan's elite. Trust me, appearances are everything."

"Tell that to poor Mama Schwartz."

"Poor Mama Schwartz nothing. She's got a mink and a beachfront condo in Miami—all courtesy of Junior.

With business that good, he could call himself Fido for all she cares."

It was good to see her smiling again. Ben was relieved to see the worry lines vanish from her brow. Admittedly the notion that she might be holding down a second job was something he hadn't even considered. Now that he did, it answered a few questions.

Still, she was driving herself hard—as hard as he had himself when he was starting out. He could understand what motivated that fire to succeed, that gritty determination that wouldn't let her quit even when the strength of her body wasn't up to the strength of her will. It was an admirable characteristic, and one that Ben had no intention of undermining—at least not on purpose.

"If business is booming, what makes you so sure you'll be fired?"

"That's the way the boutique is run," Kate explained. "The service there is impeccable, which means there always has to be plenty of staff on hand. Mr. R depends on us, and he pays a very good wage for the privilege. But because of that, he has no tolerance for unexplained absences. One mistake and you're out."

An employer himself, Ben found he could see both sides—as, clearly, could Kate. But it still wasn't right that his oversight should be responsible for her loss of a job.

"I could call him—" he began.

"Don't you dare!"

"This whole mix-up is my fault. It's hardly fair if you get blamed."

"I don't care. I don't want you throwing your weight around all over my life."

"If that sentence makes sense," Ben said mildly, "it's news to me."

She glared at him. "You know what I mean. Just leave it alone. I'll figure something out."

She would, too. She always had before. Everything she'd gotten in life, she'd had to work for. It wasn't that her parents wouldn't have helped; just that they didn't have much themselves. She was used to making the extra effort and beating the odds when she had to. Only once, just once, she wouldn't mind if things came a little easier.

Reaching up, Kate wound her hair into a thick coil, then flipped the baseball cap into place on top of it with the ease of a long-practiced motion. Ben watched as she shook out the down jacket and aimed her hand for the sleeve. "Going somewhere?"

She looked up, missed the sleeve and had to try again. "Of course, I'm going somewhere," she grumbled. "What do you think?"

"That you might be hungry."

That stopped her, as it was meant to.

"Are you offering me food?"

"Parker's had a roast in the pot all day."

The very thought made her mouth water. Pot roast. And here she'd been sure Ben was the lobster-and-caviar type. "With potatoes and carrots?"

"Potatoes, carrots—" he dangled the bait "—and plenty of biscuits for sopping up the gravy."

"Sounds like heaven." The jacket came off as quickly as it had gone on, and was dumped over the polished banister. "Lead me to it."

"Not so fast. Didn't your mother ever tell you it's impolite to wear a hat in the house?"

"That rule applies to men," Kate informed him. "Not women."

Ben reached up. "My house, my rules."

His fingers closed over the brim of the cap and slowly lifted, releasing the coils of hair beneath. The heavy strands tumbled down around Kate's neck. They were shiny and silky, and incredibly thick—the kind of hair a man's fingers could get lost in; the kind they'd burrow in while his lips held hers in a kiss. . . .

Softly Ben cleared his throat. It took a moment longer, but he cleared his mind, as well. This time, she hadn't stepped away from him. She hadn't protested the unexpected intimacy of the gesture at all. Even now, she simply stood, watching as if to see what he was going to do.

A flick of Ben's wrist tossed the cap on top of the coat. "You have beautiful hair. Why do you keep it hidden?"

"It gets in the way." Kate's shrug was deliberately casual. "Besides, when I'm out driving, it's much safer if fares can't see right off that I'm a woman."

Ben nodded but Kate saw his brow furrow, almost as if that bothered him. Patience was a virtue she'd learned—of necessity—to cultivate. Now it stood her in good stead as she waited for what would come next.

The way she saw it, Ben would make one of two moves: one acceptable, the other not. Only moments earlier, tension between them had hummed in the air like an electrical charge. And if the touch of his fingers had set her scalp tingling, it had been easy to see that she wasn't the only one who'd been affected.

Now Ben had a choice. Either he could follow that move with another in the same direction—in which case, Kate would be out of there like a shot. Or he could ignore that brief, heady exchange and go on from there—in which case her stomach, if not her ego, would be eternally grateful.

"Coming?" Ben started across the hall. "The dining room's this way." The easing of her shoulders wasn't lost on him. Nor was the full wattage of her smile.

"Sure," said Kate. "I'm right behind you."

Though there was a large cherrywood dining table in the center of the formal room, their places had been set at a small breakfast nook, situated beside a bay window. The beauty of the view was lost on Kate the moment she tasted Parker's pot roast. She had second helpings of everything, and thirds of the biscuits. Ben, who'd merely picked at his food, found himself enjoying her appreciation enormously.

"I'm glad to see you're not shy," he commented as Parker served coffee and her eyes lit up at the mention of éclairs.

"Who, me?" Kate added a generous dollop of cream to the cup and followed that with two teaspoonfuls of sugar. "You must be kidding."

"Oh, yes." Ben grinned. "I'd forgotten. You're the woman who nearly wrestled me to the floor over possession of a jelly doughnut."

Parker, serving the éclairs, let his eyebrows rise upward. He'd find enough reasons to stay in the room until he'd heard the answer to that.

"*And* the one who gave you half . . ."

Ben lifted his fork and cut into his éclair.

". . . even though you didn't deserve it."

Mouth full or not, Ben couldn't let that pass. "That's a matter of opinion."

"Of course," Kate said sweetly. "Isn't everything?"

Ben sent Parker a look. If he was going to get pummeled again, there was no sense having witnesses. Muttering, the houseman withdrew.

Kate lifted the éclair to her mouth and inhaled the dark, rich chocolate flavor. For now she just wanted to savor. In a second, she'd finish every bite and lick her fingers afterward.

"Go on," urged Ben. "Eat it. There are more in the kitchen."

"I don't need more." Kate took the first bite and chewed blissfully. "One is plenty. After this meal, I'm straining at my waistband as it is."

"From here, it looks like you've got room to spare."

"Some." Kate shrugged, having no intention of pursing the topic. "Besides, it was the smell that brought back memories. I once read that of all the senses, scent is the one which remains in your memory the longest."

Ben laid down his fork and spoon. Watching Kate was infinitely more entertaining then eating. "What memories does that bring back?"

"Childhood." She took another big bite and chewed slowly. "Cold afternoons, a warm kitchen, fresh pastry."

"Is your mother a good cook?"

"The best," Kate said, and then smiled. "But I guess everyone says that, don't they?"

"Not me. My mom could botch take-out."

"Poor thing. Cook's night off must have been hell."

Ben lifted his napkin and dabbed at his lips. "We didn't have a cook."

"Housekeeper?"

"Nope."

Kate eyed the unfinished pastry on Ben's plate with naked greed. "There must have been a maid."

Swallowing a smile, he slid his plate across the table. "A cleaning lady, Rosa. She came in once a week and did the heavy work. She didn't speak any English, and if cooking was one of her skills, I never saw any evidence of it."

"But I thought . . ." She'd put her foot in it, thought Kate. Feeling uncomfortable, she let her voice trail away.

"That I was born with a silver spoon in my mouth?"

"Something like that."

Ben clucked his tongue. "That's what you get for believing everything you read."

He could have been angry. Thank goodness, he was smiling. "All right, I'm sorry for making assumptions." Kate shook a finger at him. "And I don't apologize often, so count your blessings."

"Believe me, I always do." Ben cocked an eye toward her empty plate. "Are you sure you wouldn't like another éclair?"

"Positive. But it's been wonderful. Thank you."

"You're very welcome." Ben edged back his chair and crossed his legs. Kate was sipping her coffee. Its taste, he knew, had to be all but obliterated by her generous additions.

She'd mentioned her family, and that made him curious. It wasn't that he wanted to know everything about her, but he did wonder where her parents were, now that she was out on the streets of New York, working herself down to skin and bone. Was she supporting them? Did that explain her need to earn so much money? There was only one way to find out.

"The way you attacked that meal," he remarked, "I'd say it's been a while since your warm-kitchen-and-fresh-pastry days."

Kate looked up warily. "Those were childhood memories. I'm all grown up now."

"So I see." Ben nodded slowly. He wasn't about to tell her that with her bulky sweater and jeans cinched tightly at the waist, she looked like a wide-eyed waif. The image chilled him and he pushed it away. "Then I guess you're no longer living at home."

Kate shook her head. "Not for years."

Usually she discouraged personal questions, but now she couldn't bring herself to object. Thanks to Ben, she was well fed and well rested for the first time in what seemed like months. The feeling was entirely too pleasant to ruin with needless squabbling.

"I have an apartment in midtown. And a roommate, Maggie." Kate paused for a smile. "She's wild."

"I'll bet."

"A Catholic girl, convent raised, rebelling against her very proper upbringing."

"I'm sure you get along famously."

"We do."

"What about your parents?" Ben asked. "Are they still around?"

"Yes and no," Kate replied, then laughed at the expression on his face. "I mean, it depends what you're asking. Yes, they're still alive, but no, they no longer live in the area. Mom got so she couldn't take the cold anymore, and Dad decided that was a good excuse to pick up and move to Las Vegas."

He'd be willing to bet that there was precious little that was proper about Kate's upbringing. And that she wouldn't have changed a thing. "It sounds like he's a gambling man."

"He is." Kate smiled fondly. "And very good at it, too. He's always bragging that he takes home more from the casinos than he ever made at the phone company."

"Good for him," said Ben. Parker appeared at his elbow and began to clear the plates. "Warn me the next time he comes east, and I'll alert my crew down in Atlantic City."

"Your crew?" Kate looked up. "Oh, yes. I forgot. Westcon Casino and Hotel—the biggest resort on the Boardwalk."

The line was a slogan, taken right from his advertising. Ben wondered why she sounded so annoyed when she recited it.

Kate dropped her napkin on the table and stood. For a while, she'd been so relaxed, so comfortable, that she'd almost succeeded in forgetting just who exactly Ben was. He'd treated her like an engaging dinner companion and she'd responded in kind, as though this was one of those rare first dates—one with potential; one with a man she hoped to see more of.

But this wasn't a date, and Ben wasn't a man she could expect to see again. And if she'd needed anything to reinforce that point, the reminder of his status in the business world had been more than enough.

"I wouldn't be concerned," she went on stiffly. "A big win to him is probably a drop in the bucket to you."

Did she do it on purpose? Ben wondered. Her moods were more changeable than a north wind—and sometimes, just as cold. "I take it you're leaving?"

"Yes. It's about time, wouldn't you say?"

"Not at all."

He'd miss her when she was gone. Of course, he'd go back to his library and finish the work he'd started earlier. But the room would seem...somehow empty now, without her asleep upstairs.

He'd have quiet and solitude. He'd have the whole place to himself. Usually that was what he came to Wilton for. Tonight, it seemed like a poor trade-off.

"I want to thank you again for dinner," said Kate. She strode to the front hall to get her jacket and cap. She pulled them on, then turned to face him. "I'm sorry I yelled at you earlier. I'm sure I messed up your day just as badly as you messed up mine."

"Don't mention it." In spite of himself, Ben smiled. He should have known an apology from her would have its share of qualifiers. "You know, if you'd like, you're more than welcome to spend the night and make the drive back in the morning."

"No, I . . . I couldn't possibly." There was no use in even allowing herself to be tempted by the offer or wondering why he had extended it. Once she walked out Ben's door, that would be that. Finis. Kaput.

The next time she saw Benjamin West, he'd probably be on the six o'clock news, regaling the metropolitan area with details of his latest venture. Years from now, she'd point him out to her grandchildren and remember this day with pleasure. But that's all it was ever destined to be—a bittersweet memory, and nothing more.

"Besides," she added, "Arnie will be expecting me."

"You're not going to drive that blasted cab around the city tonight."

Kate's fingers grasped the doorknob. Through the leaded-glass panes on either side of the door, she could see her battered taxi, looking totally out of place in the circular drive. "Of course I am. That's what I do."

Over the years, Ben had learned to trust his instincts. He knew that if he let Kate Hallaby walk out the door, he'd never see her again. It shouldn't have made any difference to him, but it did. There was no time to analyze why. Instead, he went with his gut.

"Call New York," he said, "and quit your job. I'd like you to come and work for me."

5

KATE HAD THE DOOR OPEN before the meaning of what he'd said hit her. A blast of cold air swept into the hall. Slowly, deliberately, she braced herself against the frame and pushed the door until it swung shut. Only then did she turn to face him.

"What did you say?"

Ben knew she'd heard him. The stunned, slightly wary look in her eyes could hardly have been caused by anything else. Actually, he was feeling somewhat stunned himself. Since the ball was in his court, he might as well run with it.

"I offered you a job."

"Why?"

There were too many complicated answers to that. Ben tried the simplest. "Because you need one."

"No, I don't," Kate hedged, to give herself time to think. "Arnie will be mad, but he won't fire me."

"Bully for him." Now that they were negotiating, Ben was on firmer footing. "He knows a good deal when he's got one. A woman who's willing to work nights for wages so meager that you need a day job as well. Mr. Raphael should be so kind."

"All right, maybe my life isn't perfect right now. Why should you care?"

"Who says I do?" Ben shot back, and watched her cheeks color. "As it happens, I am in need of a driver.

The man I have is about to get married. His fiancée's been transferred and he's going with her."

"Leaving you in the lurch."

"Precisely."

Precisely, my foot, thought Kate. All Ben had to do was call an employment agency and he could have his driver replaced within hours. With the number of underlings he had, he wouldn't even have to make the call himself. Something strange was going on here. Something very strange indeed.

"How do you know I'm qualified?" she asked.

"If you can drive that sorry excuse for a taxi, I'm sure you can manage the Lincoln. You obviously don't mind driving, or you wouldn't be doing it now. And you probably know the city like the back of your hand."

He was right on all three counts, but Kate wasn't about to give him the satisfaction of telling him so. Nor was she about to give up her independence for the dubious distinction of becoming Benjamin West's driver. In fact, the offer was almost insulting. It meant that all the time she'd been enjoying Ben's company, responding to him as any woman would to an extremely attractive man, he hadn't regarded her as a woman at all, but instead as a potential addition to his staff.

And if that's how he perceived the situation, Kate decided, he could take his job and shove it.

"Your offer is very kind," she said sarcastically. "I'm sure others will jump at it. I'd hate to deny them the chance." This time, when she drew the door open, she welcomed the rush of cold air on her face. "I'd thank you again for dinner, but now that it's clear it really was just an extended job interview, I'm feeling a little less grateful."

Ben followed her out onto the porch. "Are you turning me down?"

Kate hopped down the steps before looking back. Outlined by the light from the open doorway behind him, his body looked lean and hard. Too bad, she thought. Somehow, knowing that life wasn't fair didn't make its disappointments any easier to take. "It sure sounds that way, doesn't it?"

"You haven't even asked about salary." When she started across the driveway, Ben found himself following her. "Or benefits."

"It doesn't matter." The cab's door handle was every bit as cold as she'd expected. Kate reached into the pocket of her parka and found her gloves. "I'm not interested."

"You should be."

Kate slid smoothly behind the wheel. "Are you questioning my judgment?"

"Yes." With effort, Ben clipped off the "dammit" he'd wanted to add.

Frustration lodged in his chest like a stone. Kate Hallaby had been put on earth to torment him. That was the only explanation. She hadn't a single reasonable bone in her body; nor an ounce of sense to go with it.

"Well, then, there you have it," Kate responded mildly. "You'd hardly want to hire someone with bad judgment. Nice try, but I'm sure it wouldn't work out."

She pulled the door shut with one hand and turned the key with the other. The engine caught on the second try, rumbling unsteadily while she stepped on the accelerator. As soon as she was sure it would hold without stalling, Kate shifted into Drive. The temptation to look back was compelling. She overruled the impulse and drove on.

Ben told himself that it was for the best. That by tomorrow, or maybe next week, he'd have forgotten all about her. He made a mental note to find out how Donald was doing in lining up a new driver. And he quashed the notion that for the first time in a long time, he'd met someone who didn't want anything from him.

Then he went inside and slammed the door behind him.

"DO YOU SUPPOSE that the concept of three hundred square feet means anything at all to a man like Benjamin West?"

Kate looked up from the floor where she was sitting, cross-legged, while she studied the weekend want ads. Her roommate, Maggie Jones, was standing in the doorway with an open florist's box in her arms. A mass of blossoms—lilies this time—rose up over the edge.

Kate greeted the sight with a sigh. "In a closet, probably. In an apartment, no."

"I swear, if he sends one more flower, one of us will have to go to make room for it," Maggie complained good-naturedly. The flowers had been arriving daily since Kate's return from Wilton.

The first had taken the only vase they had. Subsequent arrivals had been stashed in any receptacle handy at the time. Now they were beginning to run out of shelf space. Not only that, but in the tiny two-room apartment, the scent was overwhelming.

"I took the liberty of opening these." Maggie plopped the lilies in a milk carton, added water, then set them on the floor. "The card says the same thing, as always: 'Call me, Ben.'"

Kate gave a dismissive wave. "Throw it with the others." She'd never been one to waste her time on "If onlys." She wasn't about to start now.

"Is that all the thanks I'm going to get for hiking down four floors and back?"

"Quite possibly." Kate grinned. "Besides, you like getting flowers. You told me so yourself. You said it was romantic."

"In case you haven't noticed, none of these flowers are for me," Maggie pointed out. "Anyway, we passed romantic on Thursday. Now we're heading directly toward loony tunes."

Kate folded the paper and tossed it on the couch. "I couldn't agree more."

"Then tell him to stop."

"I'm not calling Benjamin West."

"Why not?"

"I told you why not," Kate said firmly. Her roommate had a very convenient memory loss whenever it came to things she didn't agree with. "I'm not interested in him or anything he has to say."

"You can bet if Benjamin West was after me, I'd be over at Westcon Plaza like a shot."

"Maggie, the man wants me to drive his car."

"Why quibble about the particulars? Think of it as an entry-level position."

"Entry to what?"

"That's up to you, isn't it? I mean, just how often do you suppose a man like Ben West sends flowers to a potential employee?"

Kate had asked herself the same question. Annoyed that she didn't have an answer, she snapped back,

"How should I know? Maybe it's part of his regular routine."

"Yeah, and maybe the Rolling Stones are coming to dinner."

Kate levered herself up from the floor. "Believe me, you'll be greeting Mick at the door long before I ever agree to become Ben's driver."

"The least you could do is give the man a chance."

"I gave him a chance." Kate frowned, remembering the dinner they had shared—*and* its aftermath. "Look where it got me."

"That's right, I forgot." Maggie gestured around the room. "All this abuse is just killing us. And don't forget about the offer of a job, which, I might add, you could definitely use. A real salary, benefits—"

"We never discussed any of that."

"Probably enough money to live on and put something away for school at the same time." Maggie's eyes narrowed. "You did tell him you've only got one semester left, didn't you?"

"Actually...no."

"For Pete's sake, why not?"

Kate smiled. "It didn't come up."

"Did the subject of law school come up at all?"

"Not exactly."

"Don't tell me, let me guess. You didn't have time. I mean, I can see how you wouldn't. After all, you only spent twenty-four hours with him. Forty-eight, now that would have done the trick. Or maybe even seventy-two—"

"Would you stop!" Kate tried to sound stern, but ended up giggling instead.

"Just tell me why."

"I didn't want to."

"That's not an answer."

It wasn't, and Kate knew that as well as anyone. Finally she settled for a shrug. "I don't know. If I'd told him about going to law school, it would have seemed like I didn't think I was good enough just the way I was. Like maybe I was trying to impress him—which I most definitely was not."

"Of course not," Maggie intoned. "After all, why would anyone want to impress Benjamin West?"

"Enough!" Kate stepped over the carton of lilies and strode to the closet. "One more word out of you, and I'm finding a new roommate."

"You can't," Maggie said mildly. "My name's on the lease, too."

"Then I'm moving out."

"Where? Onto the street? Even with rent control, you can barely afford to live here." Maggie watched as Kate yanked a jacket off its hanger and pulled it on. "Where are you going?"

"The Laundromat. It's my week, remember?"

"Want some company?" Without waiting for a reply, Maggie hefted up one of the two bags at the door.

"Are you going to continue to drive me crazy?" Kate grabbed the other.

"Probably." Maggie grinned. "But don't worry. One of these days you'll wise up and come around to my way of thinking."

Kate drew in a deep breath and exhaled slowly. "That," she said finally, "is what I'm afraid of."

IN A SMALLER OFFICE, the huge mahogany desk would have been overwhelming. In Ben's corner suite, it was merely another piece of furniture—albeit the most important. Though nearly every inch was covered with papers, Ben didn't consider it cluttered. He knew the whereabouts of each document, the significance of every folder. He had two buildings in progress, three deals pending, and an option on a piece of waterfront property.

He was on top of every one.

That was nothing unusual. That he had a splitting headache, was. Ben stored the file he was working on and watched his computer screen go blank. Three fingers massaged his right temple as he closed his eyes briefly. The headache was still there, throbbing with jackhammer force.

Frowning, he reached for the intercom. "Jody, do you think you could find me a couple of aspirin?"

"Sure, Mr. West. I'll be right in."

Ben rolled back his chair and stood, easing the crick from the back of his neck. It was dusk; across Manhattan lights were beginning to come on. Windows filled two walls of his office, and through them Ben could see it all.

Glittering New York, the city of endless promise. Below was Fifth Avenue, one of the finest addresses in the world. In thirty-six years, he'd come a long way. He'd sampled the best and the worst that the city had to offer. And he'd enjoyed every minute.

Ben let his gaze drift down to the street. People were hurrying in all directions. Traffic ebbed and flowed. A light changed and horns blared. He was too high up to hear the noise, but he could imagine it. The pulse of New York, loud as ever.

A bus cut into traffic and a taxi caromed around it. Ben found himself smiling at the sight. Any time now, Kate would go on duty. She'd light up her Vacant sign and join the fray. Knowing her, she'd do it with gusto.

He wondered if she'd been eating, and getting enough sleep. He wondered if she'd been out on interviews for a job, and if anyone had hired her. Though he'd intended nothing of the sort over the past six days, he'd found himself wondering about her a lot.

So he'd sent flowers, dozens of them. And he hadn't heard a thing. Hell, he should have sent steaks. At least then he'd know that her belly was full when she went to bed at night. But then she'd have known he was worried about her; and she'd probably have wondered why. How could he answer that, when he wasn't really sure himself?

One thing Ben did know: the week of silence had piqued his interest as almost nothing else could have. Somewhere along the line, she'd stopped being a thorn in his side and had become a challenge. And there was nothing he relished more.

There was a discreet knock at his door. "Come," said Ben, turning as it swung open. He was expecting his secretary, and got his assistant instead.

"I was on my way in anyway. Jody asked me to deliver these." Donald Rubin was a spare, thin man in his early forties. He wore tortoiseshell-rimmed glasses and combed his brown hair forward to cover a receding hairline. In his hand was a bottle of aspirin.

"Thanks." Ben crossed to the small bar, set in one corner. As he poured a glass of ice water from the pitcher, he realized that his headache was gone. "What did you want to see me about?"

Donald perched on the edge of Ben's desk. "The film crew downstairs from *Celebrity Showcase.* They'd like to come up."

"Not a chance."

"You told them they could film in Westcon Plaza," Donald pointed out. He knew he was fighting a losing battle, but he'd promised Morgan Peach he'd give it his best shot.

"And so they have. All the public areas have been opened to them." Ben recapped the bottle of aspirin and set it aside. "They knew the rules coming in. The business and residential parts of the building are off-limits."

"Several of your celebrity tenants have allowed them access to their apartments."

Ben shook his head at that. It never ceased to amaze him what lengths people would go to for a little publicity. In his position, lack of privacy was a given; but he'd never gone out of his way to court it.

He picked up his water and carried it back to the desk. "That's their option, of course."

"Mr. Peach thought perhaps you'd like to do the same."

Ben gave him the look the comment deserved.

"Hey, don't kill me, I'm only the messenger."

"One," remarked Ben, "who should know better."

Donald tried one last tack. "He'd be willing to settle for your office."

Ben sat down in his desk chair, tilting it back as he looked upward. "I must have hired you for your tenacity."

"That," Donald said with a smile, "and my Harvard M.B.A."

"Good. Then take that brainpower and perseverance downstairs and use it on Morgan Peach. Have him reshoot the fountain, let him dangle a camera from the escalator. Ask the musicians to play him a polka, but I want that shoot wrapped up this afternoon."

"Will do." Donald got up from the edge of the desk and started for the door. "Oh, there's one more thing."

Ben sipped at his water and waited.

"The flowers going to a—" Donald fished in his pocket and came up with a crumpled sheet of paper "—Miss Kate Hallaby. They've gone out every day this week but today. I just wanted to make sure you hadn't forgotten. I know it's late, but the florist will take the order—"

"No," Ben broke in. "I hadn't forgotten."

Donald creased the paper and replaced it. He was privy to almost every aspect of Ben's business, and to a great deal of his personal life, as well. More than colleagues, they were friends, and Donald felt comfortable enough to flash his boss a grin. "Don't tell me you're giving up?"

"Have you ever known me to before?"

"I've never known you to meet a reluctant lady."

"True." Ben frowned. "Pity, isn't it?"

"Not from where I sit." Donald's grin widened. "Who is she, anyway? Businesswoman, socialite? Hmm... Hallaby... Sounds Australian."

Ben knew he was going to enjoy this. "She's a hack."

"A what?" Donald swung around. "For a moment there, I thought you said she was a hack."

"I did. She drives a cab. I'd like her to take over Miles's shift when he leaves. Unfortunately, she has other ideas."

"I see. Well..." Donald cleared his throat, at a loss as to what to say next. At least he knew now why Ben had nixed all the candidates he'd found for the position. "I guess the flowers are a nice touch."

"I thought so."

If that wasn't the damnedest thing he had ever heard, it was certainly close. Flowers? For a lady cabbie who might or might not be joining the payroll? Donald started backing out of the room. If there were times when silence was golden, this was definitely one.

Ben observed his assistant's hasty retreat. "Don't look so concerned, Donald. If you'd like flowers, too, there'll be some on your desk in the morning."

"No, I . . ." The doorknob came into his hand. Donald grabbed it like a lifeline. "Just answer one question."

"Shoot."

"If she hasn't said yes, why'd you stop?"

Ben looked up and grinned. "Part of the art of the deal is to always keep them guessing."

Besides, he added silently, in this case it was only fair. After all, she was doing the same to him.

By MIDWEEK the cold snap ended. The temperature went up to fifty degrees—mild by New York standards. March, having blown in like a lion, was going out like a lamb.

Even though the day had cooled considerably by the time Kate picked up her cab, she rolled down the window anyway. Between the frigid winters and the hot, sticky summers, there were few enough chances to enjoy the feel of the wind in her hair, and she intended to make the most of it.

Her first fare took her over to the West Side, where she knocked around for an hour before another fare brought her back. Then it was a series of milk runs, midtown to downtown, downtown to up. Kate wedged a chunk of bubble gum in her cheek and kept her hands on the wheel, her eyes on the road. She drove in silence while a father and son loudly argued in the back seat; recommended a Thai restaurant to some visiting tourists; and watched a pair of lovebirds neck all the way back to the Plaza. All in all, it was a routine night-shift.

At midnight, she had a drop-off in the Village. Without much hope of finding a return, she scanned the quiet, brownstone-lined street. She'd just about given up when a man stepped out of the shadows and raised one arm.

As Kate braked, her gaze skimmed over him. Even in the good neighborhoods it paid to be careful. The man was short and stocky, wearing chinos and a bulky turtleneck sweater. A worn leather satchel was slung over one shoulder. By the light of the streetlamp, she saw a small diamond stud in his left ear.

Kate stopped between two parked cars and waited while he opened the back door and climbed in.

"I'm only going a coupla blocks," he said. "Hope you don't mind."

"No." Kate flipped the lever on the meter. "Where to?"

"Well, whaddaya know." The passenger grinned, leaning up toward the partition. "You're a chick."

Kate stiffened as she felt the hair on the back of her neck begin to tingle. She'd taken a course in self-defense and knew the first rule was basic. Trust your instincts—if you think something's wrong, it probably is.

Slowly, deliberately, she reached for the radio, her only link to the outside world. With effort, she kept her voice calm. "I just have to call this in, then we can be on our way."

"Don't."

The single word was chilling.

"But—"

A hand, holding a small shiny gun, appeared through the partition. It didn't look very big, Kate thought distractedly. Then again, it didn't take a very big hole to kill somebody.

"Don't argue. Don't say anything. Just give me your money."

Wordlessly, Kate unhooked the metal box from beneath the dashboard and passed it back through the partition.

"Now empty your pockets."

A key ring, her license and forty dollars in tips. It made a pitifully small pile on the seat. He reached over, swept up the cash and left the rest.

The gun motioned toward the door. "Now get out of the car."

"You've got what you wanted," Kate said firmly. Her heart was pounding wildly, but she knew that the worst thing she could do was show her fear. "Just take it and go."

"Maybe I got what I wanted, and maybe I don't." The grin was back. Clearly the mugger enjoyed the feeling of power the gun gave him. "Don't jerk me off, lady. Get out of the damn car."

"I'm just going to shift into Park," Kate said carefully. She didn't want to think about what he might want with her once she was out of the car. She didn't want to think at all.

"Just do it." He was growing impatient. If she was lucky, it might make him careless. "Then turn it off and hand me the key."

The shift was a lever on the right of the steering column. Kate grasped it with two fingers. The other two closed over the piece of string that hung there. A whistle—the loud police kind that could be heard for blocks—swung at its end.

"I'm shifting now," she told him. "Then I'm getting out."

He reached for his own door handle and Kate paused. If he put so much as one foot out on the street, she was gone. He didn't.

"I said *now*, lady."

"I'm going as fast as I can." She flipped the shift and grabbed the whistle in the same motion, closing her fist over it. A second flick with her other hand turned off the ignition and removed the key. "If you'd put that gun away, it would be easier."

His answer to that was a derisive snort and a bang on the partition with the barrel. "Out!"

As soon as her feet hit the pavement, he was beside her. One hand grabbed her arm, just above the elbow. The other took the key and slipped it into his pocket. "Don't make a sound. We're just going to take a little walk."

"Where?" Kate's teeth were chattering. It was an effort to shape the question around them. Keep him talking, she thought. Keep him thinking about something else. And keep looking for your chance.

"Over there."

An alley, guarded by a Dumpster, ran between two buildings. It was dark and deserted, and Kate knew with certainty that once he got her off the street, she'd never have a chance. He wouldn't even need the gun; he could overpower her with his strength alone. The same thought must have crossed his mind, for he took the weapon and tucked it into his belt.

Kate's breath lodged painfully in her throat. It was now or never.

Abruptly she faked a misstep and stumbled to her knees.

"What the hell—?"

"Damn pothole," Kate muttered.

He hadn't released her when she'd gone down, enabling her to pull him off balance. Kate prayed it would be enough. He yanked, hard, to jerk her back up. Before he knew what was happening she was on her feet, her heel grinding onto his instep, her doubled fist smashing upward into his nose.

She felt the crunch of solid contact as blood spurted down his front. His hands flew to his face. Kate sprinted toward the lighted center of the road. Lifting the whistle to her lips, she began to blow and didn't stop.

"Bitch!"

If he drew the gun, she'd run back to the shadows. Instead, he ran, one hand holding his nose, the other clutching her night's receipts. Shivering violently, she leaned back weakly against the side of the cab.

A police cruiser rounded the corner and pulled up beside her. The officer driving rolled down his window. "You all right?"

Slowly, still leaning against the taxi, Kate shook her head.

The policemen got out for a closer look. "You the one blowing the whistle?"

"Yeah." Kate looked up unsteadily. "That was me."

"Mind telling us what was going on?"

Haltingly, Kate explained. When she was done, they put her in the back of the patrol car and took her for a ride around the area to see if she could spot the mugger. To nobody's surprise, he was nowhere in sight.

Back at the cab, Kate admitted she no longer had the key. Shrugging as if this sort of inconvenience was nothing new, the officers pushed the taxi to one side of the road and left it. Then they took her downtown to file a report.

By the time she was finished at the precinct house, the morning sun was up. She'd told her story two more times. Arnie had been called and had sent another of his drivers over to the station with an extra key to pick up his cab. The lieutenant in charge had plied her with hot coffee and told her she'd been lucky.

Kate already knew that. But the knowledge wasn't enough to quiet the tremors still rippling through her as she took a bus back uptown. She jogged the three blocks from the bus stop to her building in record time, then ran up the four flights of stairs the same way.

When she reached the apartment, it was empty. Kate latched the double bolt and slipped on the chain. There was coffee in the pot and fresh doughnuts on the table. She helped herself to both. Then she sat down in a ladder-back chair and didn't move.

Slowly, gradually, she stopped trembling. Kate had no idea how long she sat. She only knew that it was long enough for her to admit to herself that she had done okay. She hadn't given up, and she hadn't given in. And with any luck, she'd broken the bastard's nose.

Her fear ebbed, and was replaced first by anger, then elation. She'd been mugged—become one of a million New York statistics—and had managed to get through in one piece. Arnie's loss would be covered by insurance. And though she'd miss her tips, they were nothing compared to what she might have lost.

So everything was just fine, wasn't it?

Who was she fooling? It was one thing to have warded off an attack last night. It was another entirely to face the fact that in her present job, someday, somewhere, she'd probably have to do it again.

The possibility didn't even bear thinking about.

It was time to weigh her options. Ben's offer was sitting firmly at the top of the list. It was an offer she didn't quite understand. Had he ignored the attraction that had sparked between them? Or had she imagined it? When a woman looked at a man and felt as though the earth had shifted beneath her feet, work was the last thing on her mind. The same hadn't been true for Ben, or so it seemed.

He was lucky, Kate mused, that she hadn't kicked him in the shins. Then again, so was she. Because now there was a possibility that his offer was still open. Of course, the flowers had stopped coming, so maybe it wasn't. There was only one way to find out.

At the back of the table, near the napkins and the salt-and-pepper shakers, sat a small, untidy pile of cards. Kate fingered the top one, then set it down in front of her. She followed suit with the second. By the time she'd reached the last, the line ran half the length of the table.

Call me, Ben. Call me, Ben. Call me, Ben.

Her eyes skimmed over them, every message the same. When she'd had a choice, she'd turned him down. Things had changed, however; and Kate, who prided herself on her flexibility, was determined to change with them.

She'd take Ben's offer. Not only that, but she'd be the best damn driver he'd ever had. And if the attraction she felt for him didn't fade with time—well, there was no way anybody had to know that but herself. Least of all, Mr. Benjamin All-Business West.

With a sigh, Kate brushed her arm across the table and the cards scattered. It didn't matter. She knew their message by heart.

Swallowing her pride, Kate made the call.

6

THE PHONE CONVERSATION was quick and to the point. They set up a meeting for six that evening in Ben's office.

Beyond that, there was plenty more Ben wanted to say and so he was left feeling dissatisfied after hanging up the receiver. He didn't know much about Kate Hallaby, but one thing was certain—expect the unexpected. She'd said she wanted to discuss his job offer; she hadn't said she wanted to accept it.

The meeting would tell, and it couldn't come soon enough. Especially after the week he'd had—five long days spent trying to secure the permits required to break ground at his newest construction site, a four-story nightclub on the Lower East Side. An hour fencing with Kate Hallaby seemed like just the diversion he needed.

What if she walked through his door and nothing happened? What if when he saw her again, his pulse remained steady, his handshake firm? What if he'd only imagined that sizzle in the air when they were last together?

Ben noted the meeting in his calendar. In that case, it was a good thing he really did need a driver.

KATE'S WARDROBE was limited—to say the least. Being a student required little in the way of clothing; driving a cab, even less. There were the two or three dresses that she'd worn at the boutique, but they seemed overly formal for what she had in mind. Besides, then she'd have had to drag out stockings and heels. She'd rather go naked.

Well, not exactly, she amended, settling on a pair of pleated corduroy trousers and a man's tuxedo shirt she'd picked up a thrift shop downtown. What she didn't want to do was look as though she'd tried too hard. No harder, that is, than any other aspiring chauffeur.

Kate giggled at the image of herself as a chauffeur. Somehow, it wasn't exactly her—the gleaming Lincoln, and the kowtowing that undoubtedly went with it. She wondered if the uniform featured breeches and high boots, and knew she'd never be able to keep a straight face if it did.

Would she be on call twenty-four hours a day and be driving Ben on his dates? Over time, maybe she'd even develop that starched look Parker had. In fact, she spent her whole day pondering anything and everything about the job, because it kept her mind off the very thing she didn't want to think about at all—what she was going to feel when she saw Ben again.

Nothing, she kept repeating to herself until she almost believed it.

At five fifty-five, she whisked past the reception desk in the lobby of Ben's building. A guard checked her name off a list, then showed her to a bank of private elevators at the rear. The trip upstairs was smooth and fast. Kate barely had time to appreciate the thick carpeting under her feet and the dark oak paneling on the walls. She did look in the mirror, smoothing her hair back twice before giving the cause up for lost. Ben would just have to take her as she was, and if he didn't, well, so be it.

His secretary was waiting at the elevator when the doors slid open. She was a slim blonde with the face of a model and the body of an athlete. The dress she was wearing would have paid Kate's rent for a month.

Her smile was warm and genuine. "Hi, I'm Jody," she said. "I'll take your coat, then you can go right in. Mr. West's expecting you."

Kate had braced herself for high tech. What she got instead was wood and earth tones. Jody's desk wouldn't have looked out of place in an English country estate. The large oil painting that graced the reception area was a Stubbs. Later, when she was less nervous, Kate promised herself the time to stop and admire. Now she gave the painting only a glance and went directly to Ben's office door.

He was on the phone when Kate walked in. He'd been trying unsuccessfully to wrap up the call with Mort Silverburg for five minutes—ever since Jody had stuck her head in the door and told him Kate was on her way up. Since their business on the nightclub project was concluded for the time being, Mort was rattling on about a dinner party he was hosting at the end of the week.

Ben didn't have to concentrate to murmur appropriate responses in all the right places. Instead he stood, waved Kate into the room, and mouthed silently, "I'll be right with you."

She nodded, glanced around the office, then strolled toward the darkened picture window that looked out over Fifth Avenue. In a similar circumstance, it was exactly what Ben would have done himself. His eyes followed her as she walked across the carpet, noting the determined set to her shoulders, enjoying the graceful sway of her hips.

For some reason—perhaps because that was all he'd seen her in—Ben had expected jeans. She'd chosen instead a pair of pleated pants made of corduroy so soft, it looked like crushed velvet. A cinch at her waist pulled them in tight, pegging at the ankles did the same. In between, they were just loose enough to tease his imagination.

The shirt she'd topped them with was with oversize, undoubtedly a man's. On another woman, he'd have found the combination strange. On Kate, it looked just right.

She didn't have to dress to call attention to her femininity because it shone through all by itself—even in old jeans and a bulky parka. Now, as she stood gazing out his window, she looked like about as much woman as a man could handle.

Quickly Ben wrapped up his call.

As he set down the receiver, Kate turned to face him. She'd been granted a few moments to compose herself and she'd needed them all. Perhaps she should have expected it, yet she was thoroughly unprepared for how strongly affected she was by the sight of the man in his own milieu. Before, he'd been magnetic; now he took her breath away.

Her response was all wrong. But what woman in her right mind could ignore the aura of power and virility that Ben radiated like a wave of heat? What woman would want to?

"Mr. West." She started across the office and held out her hand. "It's good to see you again."

Ben met her halfway and grasped her hand in his. Socially, he was more accustomed to greeting a woman friend by kissing her on the cheek. But then, he reminded himself firmly, this wasn't a social situation.

And what was he doing thinking about kissing her, anyway?

"I think we're regressing." His hand held hers for an extra beat before letting it drop. "Last time we were together, you called me Ben."

"Last time, I was turning down your job offer." Kate didn't add the obvious—that then they'd been on equal footing. Now, with her coming here tonight, the balance of power had shifted. "If the position's still available, I'd like to take it."

"Let's talk." Ben waved her to a chair. "Can I get you something to drink? Wine? Soda? Mineral water?"

"No. Nothing, thanks."

Ben was almost to his desk chair when he reconsidered. The desk was the largest piece of furniture in the room, because he needed the space. But it could also be intimidating, especially to someone left sitting on the other side. He grabbed the wing chair beside the couch, turned it around and sat down facing Kate.

"For starters," he said, "the position's still open. Let me tell you something about it, and then we'll see if you're still interested."

After what she'd been through the night before, Kate couldn't think of anything Ben might say that would change her mind, but she folded her hands politely in her lap and sat back to listen.

"I employ two drivers and they work in shifts. Nights are covered. What I'm looking for is someone to work days—seven in the morning to seven at night. Of course, you won't actually spend all that time driving. In fact, there are many days when I won't need you at all. But as long as I am in the city, or anywhere in the metropolitan area, during those hours, you'll be on call."

Kate nodded. "That's fine."

Ben's eyes narrowed at her response. Something was definitely up. Sitting before him, her hands neatly folded, she looked almost demure. Laughably so, since he knew for a fact that there wasn't a single demure bone in Kate Hallaby's body. He'd stated his requirements as bluntly as he knew how and all she'd done was nod. Where was the firebrand who'd driven him to distraction last week?

"As far as salary goes, I think you'll find it generous," he continued, naming a sum that made Kate gulp. "And of course, a full benefits package is included, as well."

"Of course," Kate murmured, trying not to think of the money and the changes it would make in her life.

She'd told herself that even if he offered the job, she didn't have to accept; that if the situation was as crazy as she instinctively felt it was, she was free to walk away. But how could she walk away from a job that would give her regular hours, food on the table and money to put away for law school, too? And if she didn't, how would she deal with the knowledge that she was attracted to Ben, and the resentment that he was able to wield such power over her life?

Kate made her decision. She'd deal with those problems the same way she always had in the past—one day at a time.

"Your job sounds just like what I'm looking for," she said primly. "I didn't bring a résumé but I do, as you know, have prior experience. I'm sure there must be some questions you'd like to ask me. . . ."

"Just one." Ben sat back and crossed his arms over his chest. "What made you change your mind?"

She'd thought he might ask about her driving record, or whether she was eligible to be bonded. She hadn't expected this. Kate waved a hand through the air vaguely. "Nothing, really."

"Come on," Ben scoffed. "You can do better than that."

"What do you mean?"

"Last week that tongue of yours ought to have been registered as a lethal weapon. Today, if I didn't know better, I'd swear you'd come here straight from the convent. What's going on?"

Coming had been hard enough. She didn't need Ben making it any harder. "Maybe I'm trying to make a good impression," she retorted.

"Hell." Ben stood, raking his fingers through his hair. "You made a great impression last week, and then you as much as told me to go jump. So, what's changed since then?"

"Nothing—"

"Did Arnie fire you, after all?"

"No." Staring down intently into her lap, Kate sensed Ben's presence beside her. She felt the warmth of his body close to hers, breathed in the musky aroma of a man who'd had a long day at work. She lifted her eyes and found his, only inches away. He had hunkered down in front of the chair, his hands braced on either arm.

"So tell me," he said gently. "What happened?"

She'd expected him to push, and she'd have pushed right back. Strength, she could have handled. His tenderness undid her.

"I got mugged."

"What?"

Kate glared at him. "Mugged. You know, held up at gunpoint? Robbed of all my money? Manhandled—"

"Good Lord." Ben rocked back on his heels. "When?"

"Last night. Early this morning." Kate shook her head. A hank of hair fell across her face and she left it where it lay. She didn't want to talk about this. The feelings—fear, anger, violation—were too powerful. But one look at the expression on Ben's face told her she wasn't going to have any choice.

"Were you hurt?" He wanted to put his hands on her. She looked as if she might punch him if he did. Everything about her radiated wariness. Instead, he decided to keep his distance—for now.

"No," Kate answered quietly. "There were just a few bruises, nothing major. Look, if you don't mind, could we just forget it?"

"No, we can't."

Ben scrambled to his feet. He'd been mugged twice. It was one of those things that happened on the streets of New York. But he knew there were fears and other emotions that had to be resolved afterward, and from the look of Kate, she'd suppressed hers. And what was that she'd said about being manhandled?

His gut churned. Ben kept his voice calm and said, "Tell me what happened."

Kate shook her head again. This time the hair flipped back, leaving her feeling curiously exposed. "It's not important."

"It *is*."

"All right then. It's none of your business."

Anger he could deal with. That, and the fact that the old Kate was back, guns firing. Ben placed a hand on either arm of her chair and leaned down over her. "It's that, too."

"Why? Because you want to hire me?"

"No. Because I care about you."

"Bull!" Kate shoved him aside and leaped to her feet. "You don't even know me."

"I want to."

She turned on him, her eyes flashing. "You want to hire me for a job."

"You're right," Ben admitted. "I want that, too."

"You want a lot, Mr. West."

"Ben." His voice was edged with steel. "We agreed you were going to call me Ben."

"No, you agreed. But then it is your show . . . Ben."

He ignored the sarcasm and went on. "Don't you realize that if you don't talk about what happened last night, it's just going to fester inside you?"

"Oh, I've talked about it, all right. I've talked to the police, I've talked to Arnie—"

"But not to anyone who cares about you." Ben watched as Kate began to pace. Each step she took carried her farther away. "What about your roommate—Maggie, wasn't it?"

Kate spun around. "Do you remember everything you're told?"

"The important things stick."

She didn't want to think about that, didn't even want to consider the possibility that she might be important to him. Kate found herself back at the window. She stared at the view and saw nothing. Maybe if she gave him what he asked for, he'd leave her alone. And that was what she wanted, wasn't it?

"He was a fare," she said quietly. "I picked him up down in the Village. He looked safe enough."

Ben's hands curled into fists at his side. He'd always thought of himself as a practical man, one who believed in accepting what needed to be done and getting on with it. But the picture of Kate going out on the streets at night and cruising for fares who "looked safe enough" filled him with anger.

"Anyway, to make a long story short, I was wrong. He had a gun and he pulled it on me. He demanded all my money."

"Which you gave to him."

Kate glanced up and found that Ben was now standing beside her. "I'm not stupid."

"I never said you were." He wanted badly to touch her. He also knew how big a mistake that would be. "Did he leave then?"

"No, it turned out he wanted something more."

There was a long silence. Reluctantly, Ben broke it. "You said you weren't hurt."

Kate shrugged and hurried on, anxious to get it over with. "He told me to get out of the cab. There was an alley...dark, empty. I knew once we got there, I was lost."

Ben nodded. He envisioned the scene in his mind and he didn't like it one bit.

"I pretended to stumble. Luckily he wasn't too bright." Kate's laugh held little mirth. "While he was off balance, I hit him, maybe broke his nose. Then I ran. The police heard my whistle, and they came. That's all there was to it."

The details were sketchy, but he got the gist. "You fought him off."

"More or less." Kate frowned. "He got away with all the money."

"Money is replaceable, you're not."

"Tell that to Arnie."

"Don't belittle yourself, Kate," Ben told her. "You don't deserve it."

She spun on him. He was standing so close that their shoulders bumped. "Listen, don't make such an issue out of it. It's no big deal. Okay?"

Ben's hand reached up. Two fingers came to rest beneath her chin. Slowly he lifted her face to his. "If it's no big deal, why aren't you out driving tonight? What are you doing here instead?"

"I knew this was a stupid idea." Kate jerked back. "I never should have come." She turned and started for the door. "I never should have believed that you actually might hire me."

"The job's yours if you want it."

The quiet sound of his voice seemed to fill the room. Kate paused as its message echoed in her head. "You wouldn't hire someone who did nothing but fight with you," she ventured.

"I might."

"Why?"

He'd asked that question often enough himself, and though he was a firm believer in common sense, there wasn't any to the answer he'd gotten. Instead, he found himself hedging. "You're a damn fine driver, Kate."

She cocked her head to one side skeptically. "Good drivers are a dime a dozen."

"Not ones I want to look at all day."

Kate's eyebrow lifted. "You're hiring me for my looks?"

Ben saw the trap coming, but he couldn't seem to avoid it. "Among other things."

"What other things?"

Step by step she came closer. There was a defiant swagger to her stride that just dared him to back away.

Ben didn't even consider the option. "Let's just leave it at that, okay?"

"And if it isn't?"

Ben shook his head. He had known this wasn't going to be easy. He hadn't considered the idea that it might be impossible. "I'm not in the habit of answering to my employees, Kate."

"Fine." She crossed her arms over her chest. "I'm not one of your employees . . . yet."

"Don't push me," Ben growled.

He looked carefully at her face, at her clear blue eyes and small, upturned nose so much at odds with the arrogant thrust of her chin. And her mouth, the full lips bare of gloss, yet still incredibly enticing . . . Any minute now, he would go over the edge. When he did, he'd make damn sure that Kate went with him.

"Or else what?" she asked.

It was the last straw. At least that's what Ben told himself. Maybe he was looking for an excuse, and maybe he'd just found it. Their first kiss had had a dreamy quality—he'd certainly dreamed about it often enough since. This time, they were both going in with their eyes wide open.

"Or else this."

One stride closed the gap between them. A second fitted her into his arms. Kate gasped, swallowing the small sound deep in her throat. Instinctively she tilted her face upward. It was all the encouragement Ben needed.

His lips found hers and moved over them. One hand nestled at the small of her back, the other burrowed through her hair. Kate knew she ought to step away. Instead she opened her mouth and welcomed him to her.

There was a familiarity to the way their bodies fit together. Kate puzzled over it only briefly before the taste of Ben filled her senses and the power of his kiss turned her knees to mush. Then her hands slid up his arms and held on tightly. If the kiss was madness, not taking full advantage of it would be a sin.

He's expected Kate to protest—maybe even counted on it. Instead she'd drawn him to her with a passion that blotted out everything save the pleasure of holding her in his arms.

Her breasts were crushed against his chest. Ben felt them through the thin cotton of his shirt. He wanted them in his hands. He wanted to lower Kate to the carpet and take her right here. He wanted to know all there was to know about her—so that he could discover what it was that made it impossible for him to put her out of his mind.

But as his hands moved to the buttons on the front of her shirt, Kate covered them with her own. Ben lifted his head and saw that her cheeks were flushed, her lips red and moist. Her voice was shaky, almost breathless, but the word it uttered was firm. "No."

For a long moment, Ben didn't move at all. Then, slowly, his hands dropped away. Shaking his head, he stepped back and gave her room. "You're right," he said quietly.

Right? Kate raged silently, torn between practicality and frustration. Who wanted to be right? The least he could have done was argue the point. Lord knew he'd argued everything else.

Frowning, she refastened the button his fingers had undone. For good measure, she did the one above that, as well. "So," she said, "is this why you offered me a job?"

"In part."

"In part," Kate muttered. She wanted to lash out at him, but how could she when what had just happened was part of the reason that she was there, too? "You didn't have to offer to pay me, you know."

Ben swung around. "I'll be paying you to drive, Kate. Nothing more."

Sure, thought Kate. When pigs fly! She glared up at him. "Asking me out would have been easier."

"You don't need a date," Ben snapped. "You need a job."

What he said made sense. The only problem was that Kate wasn't feeling even remotely sensible. "What I don't need is a man in my life calling all the shots."

"Fine." Ben spread his hands. "Nobody's forcing you to stay."

"Are you asking me to leave?"

"I'm telling you to do whatever you want. The choice is yours, as is the job if you still want it. If not . . ." Ben understood the art of negotiation, and knew when it paid to bluff like crazy. As long as she didn't figure out what was going on, he had a chance.

Kate considered it for several minutes. At the end, the situation seemed no clearer than it had in the beginning. Ben had her between a rock and a hard place. If she left, she went with nothing. If she stayed, well . . . what happened then remained to be seen.

"I'll take the job," she said finally. "On one condition."

"Which is?"

"I'm not . . . We won't . . ." Kate struggled to find the right words. "You can't have it both ways."

"All right."

"All right? That's all you have to say?"

"You set your condition, I'm agreeing to it." Ben held back a smile. The heat of Kate's passion matched that of her temper. How long this condition lasted would be anybody's guess.

"Then I guess that's settled," Kate said huffily. She should have been pleased. Instead she was feeling anything but.

"It seems that way." Ben walked over to his desk, pulled out a piece of paper and wrote something down. "Call this number in the morning. Donald's my assistant. You can work out all the particulars with him."

"Fine." As she took the paper and shoved it into her purse, Kate marveled at how quickly Ben was able to change gears. Her body was still vibrating from that incredible kiss they had shared. Ben, on the other hand, was looking every bit as starched as his shirt. "I guess I may as well be going, then."

"Let me walk you down."

"That isn't necessary—"

"I'd feel better," Ben said firmly. He took Kate's elbow and steered her toward the door. "The building's probably just about empty by now. And the streets are dark—"

"They usually are at night." Kate tried in vain to work herself up into a pique. Independence was a fine thing, but a little bit of cosseting never hurt, either.

Ben didn't even bother to reply. He retrieved Kate's coat from the closet in the reception area, held it while she slipped her arms into the sleeves, and then walked her to the elevator. He'd escort her to the curb, he decided as the doors slid shut. He'd put her in a cab, then head back upstairs.

But somehow, the closer they came to the lobby, the more reluctant he was to let her go. Even knowing that by next week she'd be in his employ and they'd be thrown together constantly did nothing to quell the urge to have more time with her—now, tonight.

Damn the paperwork he'd planned to get to. It could wait.

"Hungry?" Ben asked as the elevator doors slid open at the ground floor.

"Always." Kate looked up, startled, as the word slipped out. "I mean—"

"No problem," Ben said smoothly. "I'm starved myself. There's a deli next door that serves a mean pastrami on rye."

Kate smiled at that, but only for a moment, recalling the conditions she had just set for their relationship—conditions Ben had agreed to all too readily. True, co-workers ate together all the time, but when they did, they went Dutch. Which brought her to the subject of the tips she'd lost the night before and the two forlorn dollars that were now sitting in her wallet. At a deli in this neighborhood, that wouldn't even be enough to get her in the door.

"I'd love to," she told him honestly, "but I can't. After last night, I'm a little low on cash."

Ben nodded to the doorman as they stepped out onto the sidewalk. "Don't worry, it's my treat."

"I couldn't possibly..." Ben swung open the door to the deli, releasing a delicious medley of aromas, and Kate's voice trailed away.

"Right," he agreed, grinning at her blissful expression. "You couldn't possibly refuse."

They joined the end of the short line, and then the debate began. Ben settled on pastrami, but with the counter man pushing corned beef, Kate opted for that instead. It was macaroni salad versus coleslaw, Heineken beer versus draft.

Even after they found a table and dug into the food, the arguing continued, punctuated by much laughter. They didn't agree on movies, politics, or even sports. They went back for seconds of beer, and then another sandwich, which they split between them. The few tables in the back of the deli emptied and stayed that way. Ben and Kate didn't even notice. They ordered another round, then moved on to dessert.

By nine, the Closed sign was up and the deli man was wiping down the counters. At nine-thirty the cleaner arrived to do the floors. The sound of chairs being piled on the tables finally made them conscious of how much time had passed.

Laughing, they paid the bill and left a big tip. Out on Fifth, New York glittered before them. Streetlamps struck golden highlights in Kate's long hair, her blue eyes shone with excitement. Ben started to reach for her, then quickly recovered. His hand went up instead, to snare a cab.

"I can't afford this," Kate said as the taxi nudged in toward the curb.

Ben opened the rear door. "I can."

Kate hesitated. Especially at this time of night, it was a much more enticing alternative than the subway. Which didn't mean she had any intention of getting used to having Ben paying her way. "Maybe I could have an advance on my salary?" she suggested. "A small one?"

"Of course." Ben took out a ten-dollar bill and folded it into her hand. He'd have been happy to pick up the fare, but he also could appreciate pride when he saw it.

"Thanks." Kate's eyes met his, but then it was she who was held mesmerized by his strangely intimate look. "For everything."

"My pleasure."

Ben helped her into the cab, gave the address to the driver. No sooner had she pulled the door shut than the taxi took off into the traffic. The last thing Ben saw was Kate giving him a jaunty wave through the rear window. He lifted his hand to return the salute, but the cab was already gone.

Suddenly aware of the cold night air, Ben reentered the Westcon Plaza lobby. He started for the commercial elevators, then headed for the residential bank instead. Though there was work to be done, he had no desire to go back to his office.

He wasn't in the mood, and the notion made him smile. When was the last time he'd considered what sort of mood he was in? Not recently, that was for sure.

But somehow, after the time he'd spent with Kate, it seemed to matter. Other women deferred to his needs, tiptoed around him as if he were made of glass. Kate, on the other hand, was just Kate. Just by her very presence—enticing, abrasive, frustrating as hell—she managed to drag him down out of his glass tower. Even his most pressing issues took on a whole new perspective. But was she good for him? He didn't have a clue. One thing, however, he did know—hiring her was either a stroke of genius, or else the dumbest idea he'd ever had in his life.

7

"YOU CAN'T QUIT ON ME, doll." Arnie's thick Brooklyn accent came through the telephone line loud and clear. "Trust me! A few days off and you'll be good as new."

"I'm good as new now," Kate insisted patiently. The conversation was a repeat of one they'd had every day for the last three—ever since the night she'd accepted Ben's offer and tried to quit her old job. "I just don't want to go back to driving nights, or picking up strangers."

"Of course not," Arnie agreed. "I can see that."

Right, thought Kate. Nothing she'd said during their two previous discussions had made the slightest impression on him, so why should this? On the other hand, though Arnie hadn't been the easiest boss, he had, for the most part, been fair. If it took a little extra effort to disengage herself, Kate could hardly begrudge him that.

"Days," he suggested determinedly. "Maybe I could fit you into the roster."

"Thanks, but no thanks." Kate looked over at Maggie and rolled her eyes. "I've already got a day job. Put an ad in the paper, Arnie. Somebody will turn up."

"Yeah, but I like you. You're smart, you speak English, and you don't talk back. On top of that, you're hungry. In other words, the perfect hack."

"Why, Arnie," Kate cooed, "if I'd known how much you appreciated me, I'd have asked for a raise."

"Don't go gettin' wise on me," Arnie retorted. "Look, I gotta go. Days—think about it."

Kate grimaced as the line went dead.

"I take it Mr. Personality is still on your case?" Maggie asked from across the room.

Kate nodded as she replaced the receiver. "He just can't understand why I would want to quit an august establishment like his."

"Nice to be popular."

"Ain't it." Kate walked over to the refrigerator and poured herself a glass of orange juice. "Speaking of which, where's Josh tonight? I can't remember the last time you two didn't spend a weekend together."

"On his way to Puerto Rico," Maggie said with a sigh. "Business. He'll be back Wednesday."

"Poor thing. Dateless on a Sunday night. What is the world coming to?"

Maggie picked up a pillow and threw it at her. "You're a fine one to talk. You haven't had a date in months."

"I haven't had a free moment in months."

"You had plenty of time when Barry was around."

Kate felt her shoulders stiffen. "I was in school then."

"So you were." Maggie studied her fingernails with great interest. "One day he was around, the next he was gone. You never did tell me why."

An image of Barry floated before Kate's eyes—blond and gorgeous with his perpetual tan and boyish grin. They'd been students together—Barry had graduated in January. For a time last winter, she'd believed she was in love, and maybe she had been. But that hadn't stopped him from leaving her.

"Let's just say that Barry liked me more as a lawyer-to-be than he did as a struggling cabbie."

Maggie looked up in surprise. "Wasn't he the one who was always spouting rhetoric about a classless society?"

Though the remark deserved a smile, Kate couldn't even come close. Instead she nodded. "The sentiment went along with the rest of his ambitions: pass the bar, clerk for some well-placed judge and then zoom straight into politics, with Gracie Mansion being the eventual goal. He didn't mind that I wanted to go into legal aid. After all, these days it has a certain cachet. Then he was graduating, and I was dropping out. Suddenly we weren't a match made in heaven anymore."

The intercom by the door gave a loud squawk. Relieved by the interruption, Kate got up to answer it.

"Delivery for Miss Kate Hallaby."

"I'll be right down."

"No need. I'll bring it up. Four C, right?"

As Kate pressed the button and opened the door, Maggie came to stand beside her. "You don't suppose it's more flowers, do you?"

"Worse. When I talked to Ben's assistant last week, he took my measurements and said he'd send over some uniforms."

"Really?" Maggie giggled. She skipped out into the hall and leaned down to look over the railing. The deliveryman was on the third landing. "Hurry up!" she cried gleefully. "Let's see what you've got."

While Kate took care of the tip, Maggie snatched the box and carried it into the apartment. "This is just like Catholic school," she chortled.

"I hope not." Tearing off the wrapper, Kate found three pairs of black wool pants, two matching jackets, six crisp white shirts, and a dozen pairs of lisle socks.

"What?" asked Maggie. "No underwear?"

At the bottom of the package was a smaller box, nestled within the tissue paper. It contained a cap—flat, black, and narrow-billed. Grinning, Kate scooped her hair up under it and ran to look in the mirror.

"Not bad," Maggie decided, following her into the bathroom.

"Not great, either." Kate turned her head from side to side, studying the effect. "It needs something...."

"Like maybe a Yankees emblem on the front?"

"That would do."

Maggie watched as Kate flipped the cap off and sent it sailing across the room. "Now that you're all outfitted, when do you start?"

"Tomorrow morning, seven o'clock sharp."

"Seven?" Maggie squeaked. Her job at the New York Public Library didn't start until nine. If she rushed, she could sleep until eight.

"That's when my shift begins. I go to the garage, make sure the car's in order, and await further instructions."

"What if there aren't any?"

"Then I'll be bored—" Kate smiled self-deprecatingly "—like good flunkies everywhere."

Maggie's expression grew thoughtful. "Is that really how you see yourself, as Benjamin West's flunky?"

"No," Kate answered quickly. "But then that hardly matters, does it? What matters is how Benjamin West sees me."

BEN WAS A CREATURE of habit—always had been, always would be. He woke each morning promptly at six, his own internal alarm clock propelling him up and out of bed. The next half hour was devoted to working out. In the country, he ran; in the city, weights and Nautilus equipment had to make do. By six forty-five, he was showered, shaved and dressed. Parker served his first cup of coffee with the *Wall Street Journal,* the second with the *New York Times.* Ben shoveled down breakfast while he devoured them both.

By seven-fifteen, he would be downstairs in his office. Most mornings, Donald arrived at eight, Jody at nine. Ben relished the time alone. The phones were quiet, as were the halls. There was no sound at all save the hum of his computer as he organized his day.

Monday morning found Ben behind his desk as usual. His calendar was open to the correct page, his appointments neatly noted. His first meeting was scheduled for ten, at his office. Four others followed hourly.

Midafternoon, he and Donald were heading out to Queens to look at a piece of property near the airport. At five o'clock, Mort Silverburg was due. At six, he was having cocktails with the mayor and various other luminaries at the opening of a new exhibit at the Museum of Modern Art. It was a normal day, no different from the others that had preceded it.

And it was Kate's first day on the job.

He shouldn't have been thinking about her. But knowing something and acting on it were proving—in Kate's case—to be two entirely different things. By now, Ben mused, she would be down at the garage, probably talking to the day man and drinking stale, machine-bought coffee. She'd be wearing the uniform Donald had undoubtedly provided—solemn, black and unobtrusive. Except that Kate Hallaby wouldn't be unobtrusive in a shroud.

Unfortunately he wouldn't have a damn thing for her to do until afternoon. He wondered if she'd grow restless with the waiting. In her position, Lord knows, he would.

But then he wasn't in her position, Ben reminded himself firmly. He was the man in charge, setting his own schedule, making his own decisions . . . and feeling restless as hell.

With an oath, he got up from behind the desk. Maybe he'd been working too hard. It was a sure bet something was wrong when he looked at his calendar—filled with the names of some of the most important people in the city—and felt nothing but obligation. Ben tilted his wrist and glanced at his watch: seven-thirty. There was still plenty of time before his first meeting. And when was the last time he'd enjoyed an early-morning walk?

By the time he reached the lobby, Ben had accepted the fact that he was going to see Kate. That done, he figured he might as well stop at the deli and pick up breakfast. No matter that he'd already eaten; Kate was fully capable of eating for two, or maybe three if it came right down to it.

The garage was three blocks east, Ben knew, though he'd never been there before. When he wanted the car, it simply came to him. Now he made the walk in five minutes. As he strode in the open entryway, the attendant glanced at him with no sign of recognition.

"I'd like the West Lincoln," Ben announced.

That got the man's attention. "We didn't get no call," he said. "We always get a call."

"Not this time." Ben's gaze swept around the drafty lot. "Where's my driver?"

"He's . . . uh, she's in the lounge."

It was an overstatement if he'd ever heard one. The small, dank, cheerless room where Kate sat, her nose buried in a thick book, no more resembled a lounge than a wooden dinghy resembled the *Queen Mary*. As he pushed open the door, Kate glanced up. Her eyes widened, then she shoved the book behind her and leaped to her feet.

"Ben! I mean, Mr. West... What are you doing here?"

Hastily Kate composed herself, ignoring the tiny flip-flop of her heart. She'd thought she'd have some warning before seeing him again, a chance to school her features into the bland mask that the job required. But here he was, looking gorgeous in an English-tailored suit and wind-ruffled hair, and she wasn't prepared in the slightest.

She buttoned her jacket, smoothed a hand over her hair. "They told me you'd call if you wanted the car. I haven't missed something already, have I?"

Ben shook his head slowly, watching her reaction, taking it all in. His first feeling had been one of anger. She didn't belong in these surroundings. She wasn't just some anonymous driver; she was ... Kate, a woman whose place he'd be hard-pressed to define, although he knew for certain this wasn't it.

But his irritation ebbed, to be replaced by a wave of pleasure at simply seeing her again. Ben didn't have to define that. All he had to do was enjoy it.

"I don't understand..." Kate began, but Ben held up his hand.

"Have you eaten?"

She eyed the bag in his hand. "Why are you always asking me that?"

Ben grinned. "Because you're always hungry. Come on, I've had the car brought up. We're going out for a drive."

He spun on his heel and headed back toward the office. Throwing dignity to the winds, Kate scrambled to catch up. "Where are we going?"

"Out."

"Out where?"

"Has anyone ever told you that you ask too many questions?"

The Lincoln was idling in the entrance. Kate managed to get in front of Ben just in time to open the rear door. To her annoyance, he walked right past her and let himself in the passenger side of the front.

She glared at him and hurried around to her own door. "How do you expect me to drive you if I don't know where we're going?"

Ben smiled complacently. "Fake it."

She'd been on the job less than five minutes, Kate reflected as she slipped in behind the steering wheel, and she'd already discovered its biggest drawback: She couldn't punch the man in the nose when he deserved it.

Instead she looked both ways, then pulled out into traffic. The street headed west, so she did, too. At Fifth, she turned and drove north, passing the Plaza before skimming along beside Central Park. Ben remained silent.

Stopped at a red light, Kate gave him a sidelong look. She wasn't used to feeling this off-balance. Until she'd met Ben, she'd known exactly who she was and where she was going. She'd been in control. Now what came next was anybody's guess. Every time he looked in her direction, she felt edgy; her face flushed and her heart pounded—and it was all Ben's fault.

"You know," Kate said grumpily, "you're supposed to be sitting in the back."

"I know."

Well, *that* hadn't solved anything. This time, the look she gave him was closer to a glare. "You gave me this job, Ben, and I intend to do it right. But how can I behave in a professional manner if you don't?"

So she was back to using his first name again. Ben held back a smile. That was progress. Or else she was too put out by his behavior to notice she'd done it.

"You're in the middle lane, in heavy traffic," he pointed out, his voice tinged with what sounded suspiciously like amusement. "Would you like me to climb over the seat?"

"You could try."

Ben eyed the narrow space between seat and ceiling. "You'd enjoy that."

Kate didn't mean to laugh, but she couldn't seem to help it. "Probably."

"I hate to deny you the pleasure, but I've got a better idea." He pointed suddenly toward an opening into the park at the next corner. "Turn left."

Kate spun the wheel and careened across the lanes of oncoming traffic. The Lincoln shot onto the access road. Horns blared in their wake.

Ben righted himself in his seat. "Most people," he said, "drive a limousine with more finesse than a cab."

"Most people," Kate replied sweetly, "get better than two seconds' notice. Now what?"

"Park somewhere. Anywhere at all."

"Yes, sir."

Kate drove for another minute before edging the big car over to the curb and cutting the engine. The spot she'd chosen was quiet, the road surrounded on either side by lush green fields. Even at that hour of the morning, the park was in use. Joggers and dog walkers were all around. But though the Manhattan skyline was clearly visible over the tops of the trees, the bustle of the city seemed very far away.

"Well," asked Kate, turning in her seat, "did I pass the driving test?"

Lord knows why she attracted him. He'd never met a woman who got under his skin so easily. Or who seemed to enjoy doing it so much. "Barely."

"Great." Kate smiled. "Now can we eat?"

Well, maybe he did know why she attracted him. And that sassy grin had plenty to do with it. As did her long legs and a sexy rear end that wasn't half done justice by the somber uniform.

"We'd better," Ben said, opening the bag. "If you're going to drive the same way you got us here, I'm going to need all my strength."

Kate had a retort ready, but it died on her lips when she saw the bounty Ben spread on the seat between them. Onion bagels, cream cheese, lox, and several kinds of fresh fruit. For a breakfast like this, she'd be more than happy to call a truce.

"There's butter, too." Ben reached down into the bottom of the bag and pulled out the last few things.

"Sacrilege!" said Kate, spreading cream cheese liberally over her bagel.

"That's what Nico said." Ben picked up a bagel and followed her lead.

"Who's he?"

"The owner of the deli. He said if you didn't know the correct way to enjoy a New York bagel I should bring you back and he'd show you himself."

"Oh, he did, did he?" A smear of cream cheese ran along her upper lip. Kate cleaned it off with her tongue.

"Uh-hmm." For the moment, watching her, it was all the sound Ben could manage. He couldn't have it both ways, she'd told him. He wondered how she'd respond to being fired.

"He also said you were cute."

"He did?" Kate looked up, pleased.

Ben picked up a peach and sank his teeth into the soft skin. He'd rather have had them on her lip. "When I told him that we just worked together, he asked me for your phone number."

Kate's brow lifted.

"For Nico, Jr."

She swallowed a bite of bagel that went down with a gulp. "Nico, Jr.?"

"His son." He couldn't touch her. But that didn't mean he couldn't provoke a response. "He's a nice Greek boy, helps out his father in the deli." He polished off the peach and nonchalantly went about spreading cream cheese on another bagel.

"So?" Kate demanded.

"So what?"

She'd never have believed that anyone with features as strong as Ben's could contrive to look so innocent. "Did you give it to him?"

"Of course not. I told him I didn't know whether you were involved with anyone or not."

"Thank God."

"So—" Ben hesitated "—are you?"

Kate cocked her head to one side and considered the question. More specifically, she considered the reason Ben had asked it. "What does that have to do with my job?"

His eyes were a dark, bittersweet-chocolate shade of brown. In the moment's pause, she felt her breath catch in her throat. He'd made no move to touch her but she put her hands up anyway, warding off . . . she didn't know exactly what.

"What," Kate repeated in a ragged whisper, "does that have to do with my job?"

"Nothing."

It was what she was afraid of, and, at the same time, what she wanted to hear. And because she couldn't deal with both emotions at once, Kate dismissed them. She squared her shoulders and thrust out her chin. "Then you have no right to ask."

With unhurried and supremely confident movements, Ben laid a piece of salmon on the last bite of bagel. "I'm asking anyway."

"And if I chose not to answer you?"

"I'll find out."

Kate swallowed a frustrated growl. "Do you always get what you want?"

"Eventually."

She wanted to be angry, but damn the man, he was probably right. And she could hardly condemn him for telling the truth. Instead she struck back. "How about you? Do you have a girlfriend?"

"Fair is fair." Ben smiled. "I'll answer your question if you answer mine."

"Done."

"All right, then. I have women friends that I see from time to time, but I'm not involved with anyone special. I suppose I'd like to be, but I'm not."

Kate set her bagel aside. "Why would you like to be?"

"I'm thirty-six years old, Kate. That's the age when a man stops counting his successes and starts wondering who he's going to share them with." Ben glanced at her. "Despite what you think, I'm a perfectly normal man. I'd like to have a wife and children—now, before I get too much older."

She wasn't going to think about his children, Kate told herself firmly. Nor the gorgeous blonde who would undoubtedly provide them. "So what's stopping you?"

"The same thing that stops everyone else." There was a hint of irritation in his voice. He wasn't accustomed to answering personal questions, and it showed. "I haven't fallen in love."

"Is that so important?"

Ben was gathering the paper wrappings and putting them back in the bag. It was a long moment before he spoke. "Are you really such a cynic, Kate? Or is that an act you put on for my benefit?"

Stung, she shot back a reply, "I don't do anything for your benefit."

"Somehow," Ben said dryly, "that doesn't surprise me."

Kate looked away, biting down hard on her lower lip. She'd hurt Ben's feelings, and she hadn't meant to. All she'd wanted was to keep their conversation light, and she'd succeeded too well.

Even when Ben had answered her questions—questions she had no right to ask—she persisted in being flip and smug. That she'd done it in self-defense was hardly an excuse. Ben was becoming her friend, and he deserved better.

Kate gazed out the side window of the car. In the open field, a young man tossed a Frisbee for his dog. The animal streaked after it before leaping into the air for a spectacular flying catch.

Unexpectedly, Kate felt a kinship with the pair. It was scary racing headlong after something when you had no idea where you might end up. Scary—and exhilarating.

"Maybe it's an act," she said quietly.

Ben paused in the midst of rewrapping the extra food, and looked up. "What?"

"I said maybe it's an act. Or maybe I've tried so hard to be tough for so long, that now that's the way I really am."

Ben reached over and placed his hand on top of hers. Her fingers, slim and strong, nestled in his palm. There was strength there, but with it came vulnerability. He remembered how she'd felt that first night, sleeping in his arms. How long would it be before he held her that way again?

"New York is a tough town," he said. "And anyone who wants to make it here has to be just as tough. You're a survivor, Kate. Be proud of that. There aren't many people who can say the same."

Kate swallowed a sigh at his words. So she was a survivor, was she? Fat lot of good that did her, sitting next to a man who was used to debutantes. She wanted to believe what he said about being proud. Or maybe she just wanted to sit there a little longer and enjoy the feeling of her hand in his.

"So what made Benjamin West so tough?" she asked.

"I was born that way."

Kate traced a forefinger across his wrist and enjoyed watching him start. "No, you weren't."

"Corrupted at an early age?"

"Maybe."

"Ben?"

"Hmm?"

"Tell me about the O'Dwyer Building."

He sat up at that. "What do you mean?"

"I went to the library last week. You know, prospective employee reading up on the new boss? From the periodicals I read, it seems that what happened there isn't your usual way of doing business."

"You want to give me a second chance?" Ben asked.

Kate shook her head uncomfortably. "Maybe I want to apologize."

"Maybe?"

"I haven't heard your side yet."

"I see." Ben withdrew his hand. Her opinion mattered to him. Why else would he be considering telling her a story he'd never told anyone else?

"Everything went wrong there," Kate pointed out. "Yet the building had your name on it."

"No." Ben looked up. "My father's name."

Confronted by a possibility she'd never even considered, Kate was silent for a moment, then quietly asked, "Your father's in construction, too?"

"He was. West Development was his company, not mine."

"But if you had nothing to do with what happened—"

"I never said that," Ben growled. Damn if she didn't know just which buttons to push. "I had everything to do with it."

This time it was Kate who reached out to touch, laying her hand gently on his arm. "Tell me," she said softly. "Please?"

Ben sighed. He'd tried enough evasions in his day to know when one wouldn't work. "It's a long story."

"I've got time."

That's what he figured. "Fifteen years ago, I'd just joined my father's business. We bought the O'Dwyer

Building for a conversion, or so I was told. It was to have been our first project together."

"So, what went wrong?"

In spite of himself, Ben smiled. "If you keep interrupting, you'll never find out."

"Sorry."

"Anyway, it turned out my father had different plans. He knew I objected so he didn't tell me about them. One day he sent me to New Jersey on business. It's amazing how much a good wrecking crew can accomplish in a day's work—by the time I got back, the building was as good as gone."

"What did you do?"

"I confronted him." Ben frowned, remembering. "Yelled a lot. Of course, it was too late. He said there'd been a change of plan. The building was too old, too unsound, for renovation. We were going to rebuild, instead—a mixed-use complex with residential floors for those tenants who wanted to stay."

"That wasn't what happened," Kate said.

"No," Ben agreed. "It wasn't. But it was another six months until I caught him in the lie. This time he only shrugged and told me there was nothing I could do. When I went down to the Department of Records to check the papers, I found out he was right. My father was pretty savvy, I'll give him that. When I read the fine print, I found that my name was only on the O'Dwyer Building, itself. My father owned the land and the new construction. I'd put in a year's worth of work and was left with a handful of rubble."

"That's terrible!" Kate cried fiercely, thinking of her own family. They didn't have much, but what they did have was always shared. That Ben had been used was bad enough. That his own father was responsible was unconscionable. "Surely he must have seen that you were entitled to something?"

Ben found himself smiling at her vehemence. "He didn't toss me out on my ear, if that's what you're thinking. From his point of view, he'd taught me a lesson about doing business in the Big Apple—one that I needed to learn. Having done that, he bought me out. I used that stake to start my own company."

"I still think it's rotten."

Ben's smile widened. So much for his cool, unruffled chauffeur. If he'd needed any proof that she cared, she'd just handed it to him in spades. Futile though her anger was, Ben relished the fact that she'd leaped to his defense with such passion. "Don't feel sorry for me," he said. "After all, as it turned out, I haven't done too badly."

Kate declined to comment. Apparently he wasn't upset, so why should she be? Just because the picture of Ben—young and learning his business the hard way—brought a lump to her throat? Just because she was tempted to wrap her arms around him and—

Phooey, thought Kate, scooting back over to her own side of the seat. She might have apologized for having misjudged him but he didn't seem to want that, either. And that was precisely the problem: Ben didn't want anything from her—at least not what she wanted to give.

"I guess we'd better be getting back," she said briskly.

"Oh?" Ben asked, amused. "What's your hurry?"

She opened her mouth, then slowly shut it. For a moment she'd forgotten that she was there at his convenience. He gave the orders, not she. It was a fact that would take some getting used to.

"I'm sorry," Kate said, aiming for a humble tone and missing by a wide margin. "I didn't mean to presume—"

"By all means, presume away." Ben swept the last of the debris into the bag and set it on the floor. "If you think it's time to go back, you're probably right. Drop me off in front of Westcon Plaza, okay?"

They made the drive in silence, with Kate calling herself every kind of idiot as she maneuvered deftly through the traffic. At the rate things were going, she'd be lucky if she lasted a week on the job. And wouldn't Arnie have the last laugh when she came crawling back?

"Just pull over here," Ben directed as the gilded facade came into view. "I'll hop out and run across."

Kate studied their position on the wrong side of the road. "You're sure? I could go around the block—"

"Here is fine." Ben waited until he'd opened the door and swung it partway open before finally turning to face her on the seat. "You know," he said, "a deal's a deal. I answered all of your questions, and you never did get to mine. Are you free? Should I give Nico your number?"

Her heart leaped at the first part of his question, then took a dive at the second. "Yes," she responded, "and no." Her eyebrows lowered menacingly. "Most emphatically, no."

"That sounds promising." Ben grinned devilishly and Kate's hands tightened on the wheel.

"Which part?"

He slid out of the car and shut the door behind him. For a moment, Kate thought he wasn't going to answer, then he strode around to her side of the car, daring traffic as he leaned his head down to her open window. "Both."

His lips were only inches from hers. All she had to do was turn her head and raise it slightly.... The notion got only a moment's thought—upstaged by a wide-bodied truck in the right lane that was bearing down fast. "I think," she observed, "you're about to be killed."

"Nonsense," said Ben, but he straightened and had a look. "This is New York. Drivers are used to obstacles."

The trucker blasted his horn.

"This is New York," echoed Kate, "where drivers knock obstacles out of their way. I've done it."

"You haven't."

"Try me." Kate sent him a mischievous look.

The horn blared again.

Ben swore, then sprinted away through the lanes of traffic. The truck missed him by inches.

"Jaywalker!" Kate yelled after him.

He never even turned to look.

Ben entered the building and went straight to the elevators. The ride up gave him barely enough time to smooth back his hair and straighten his tie. It wasn't enough to tamp down his grin.

No sooner had the doors slid open than Jody was there, with Donald right behind her. "You're late!" she cried.

"No, I'm not." Ben looked at his watch. "It's barely nine, and I haven't got anything scheduled until ten."

"Yes, but..." Jody stammered. "I mean..." Her voice trailed away and she appealed mutely to Donald for help.

"What she means is, when we got here, you weren't in your office."

Ben looked back and forth between them. "Was it on fire?"

"No, of course not, but—"

"Then what's the problem?" Still grinning, Ben strode between them, heading for his office.

With a puzzled shrug, Jody gave up and went back to her desk. Donald hurried along in Ben's wake. "We've had a call from the casino. Cher's canceled her booking."

Ben sat down behind his desk and rolled the chair in tight. "Get someone else to fill in."

"She's our biggest draw. It'd be a shame to lose her."

"What's the issue? Money?"

Donald shook his head. "I gather there was some sort of tiff with the stage director. He's willing to apologize, but the manager thought that a personal call from you might smooth things along. . . ."

"Right." Ben pulled his calendar across the desk and made a small notation. "I'll take care of it."

"I guess that's all, then." Abruptly Donald peered at his friend. "Are you all right?"

Ben looked up. "Fine. Never better. Why?"

"I don't know. First you come in late, then I tell you that our biggest star has canceled out from under us and you don't even blink. Is there something going on that I should know about?"

"Not a thing," said Ben, his tone firm enough to squelch further discussion.

As Donald let himself out, Ben ran a finger down the agenda in his calendar, noting the names and the times, and hummed with renewed vigor at the prospect. Maybe it wasn't going to be such a bad day after all.

8

WITH APRIL, CAME RAIN: a series of cool, overcast days that belied the promise of spring. Clouds hung low over the Manhattan skyline, shrouding the buildings in a damp, gray mist. The sidewalk vendors put away their gold chains and hawked umbrellas instead. With their customary élan, New Yorkers coped with adversity by ignoring it.

It had to be the weather, Kate told herself. That's why Ben was calling for the car so often. After all, Donald had warned her from the start that she would spend a great deal of time doing nothing, because their boss preferred walking when possible. Two weeks into the job, the long, boring days she'd anticipated never materialized. Instead, her shifts were filled with interesting things to do, from picking up visiting dignitaries at the airport to chasing down the perfect box of Belgian chocolates. And then there was the mainstay of the job—ferrying Ben back and forth on his numerous appointments.

There were far worse ways to make a living.

And if she was still ambivalent about being Ben's employee, Kate kept her feelings firmly under wraps. She'd known from the beginning that the attraction she felt for Ben was impossible: known and accepted it, as she'd accepted other disappointments in the past.

Kate had never been one to dwell on what couldn't be, and she wasn't about to start now. Instead she concentrated on enjoying what she had. The job was interesting, well paid, and safe. Not only that, but she got to spend a good part of each day in Ben's company.

Like all employers, he had his quirks. Chief among them was an intense dislike for posturing and pretension. When Ben was riding with his associates, he sat in the back, often conducting business as Kate drove. When he was by himself, however, he climbed in the front with her—talking, gesturing, and providing Kate with all manner of distractions.

He also, she discovered, had a penchant for thinking out loud. It was not unusual for him to pull out blueprints for new real estate, or run through the steps of a planned conversion while Kate was at the wheel. She listened, fascinated, while he described the inner workings of a business whose vast scope she was only beginning to comprehend.

And, it was not unusual for her to tell him exactly what she thought of his plans. She considered Westcon Tower a masterpiece of Art Deco architecture; the land near the airport—which Ben had declined—a steal he'd regret missing, and the nightclub proposal a waste of time and money in a city already overburdened with "in" spots.

Ben listened, encouraging her to speak up and say whatever was on her mind. More than once, Kate reflected with pleasure, he'd even conceded the points she'd made. It was one thing to have studied law, and something else entirely to see the practical applications of what she'd learned. Through his willingness to include her, Ben offered Kate priceless knowledge of real-estate acquisition and development.

The job was fresh, stimulating, and incredibly interesting—just like the man who came with it; the man who had said he only wanted her to drive his car. And if there were times when the atmosphere in the front seat of the Lincoln was just this side of combustible, then she'd learn to deal with it.

For the first time in a long time, she was waking up each morning with a smile on her face. For now, that was sufficient.

IT WAS HELL, thought Ben. Two long weeks of the sweetest torture he'd ever endured. He must have been crazy to hire Kate as his driver—there was no other excuse.

Right off, she'd piqued his curiosity and his desire. She had pluck and spirit and wit. And unlike most others, she wasn't the slightest bit intimidated by him. He'd been enticed and entertained by her. Hell, he'd been damn near entranced. How else to explain what had happened?

He should have asked her out. Even Kate had told him that. What she hadn't told him was whether or not she would have accepted. And so he had let his protective impulses overrule his libido. Though he'd never thought of himself as the nurturing sort, something about Kate knocked him for a loop. He'd wanted to take care of her. So, impulsively he'd acted on it. Now, thanks to that moment of lunacy, he was being chauffeured around town by a woman who could light his fuse without even trying.

Of course, they were totally unsuited to each other. Any idiot could see that. He'd thought the constant exposure would help get her out of his system. Instead, the opposite was happening.

Whoever would have expected her to understand the fine points of New York zoning laws or the land-use regulation system? He'd known she was smart. Still, he was floored by his discovery that her intellectual curiosity, her thirst for knowledge, rivaled his own. Day after day, Kate amazed and delighted him.

And that was precisely the problem.

That night in his office she'd asked him to choose, and he had. For a man who routinely wagered millions on a single deal, it was humiliating to admit that he'd made the wrong decision.

He recognized that she was attracted to him. Yet, as surely as she gave her temper free rein, she held her passion in check—just as he'd been forced to do ever since he'd backed himself into this ridiculous position. And if the effort wasn't wearing on her, it surely was on him.

Did she have any idea how sexy she looked in that tailored uniform? Or of how often he called for the car, when in the past he'd simply have walked? He found himself looking forward to their drives—spending time that he used to devote to reading, conversing with her—talking and, very deliberately, not touching.

The situation was untenable; that was all there was to it. He wasn't a sentimental man and never had been. In the past, when something wasn't working, he'd put an end to it. Now, he couldn't see that he had any other choice.

KATE STOOD in the reception area on the forty-second floor, staring at the closed oak door of Ben's office. It was just after seven in the evening. Jody was long gone, and she'd passed Donald in the lobby.

"He's in his office," Donald had told her. "Go right on up."

"You're sure he wanted me and not the car?" Kate asked uncertainly.

"That's what he said."

Then Donald had left and she was on her own, standing outside Ben's door. Why in the world had he summoned her? As she raised her hand to knock, the office door opened.

"Good, you're here," said Ben. "I thought I heard the elevator."

Bemused, Kate stared at him for a moment. Ben's dark hair was rumpled, his paisley tie loosened. Though presumably his suit had a jacket, it was nowhere in sight. Dark red suspenders hugged his torso, delineating the solid breadth of his chest. Pleated pants fit smoothly over his lean hips. The sleeves of his shirt were rolled back out of the way, revealing strong, well-developed forearms, covered by a dusting of dark hair.

He looked vital and incredibly sexy. The effect was like stepping out of a plane at thirty thousand feet. Kate felt her stomach plummet.

"Come on in," Ben said. Then, catching her expression, he asked, "Is something wrong?"

"No, of course not." Kate shook her head. But as she followed him into his office, she remembered the last time she'd been there and that single, heart-stopping moment when Ben had strode across the room and taken her into his arms. . . .

"You look faint," Ben said with concern. "Can I get you anything?"

"I'm fine." She blinked rapidly several times. "Really."

"If you say so." Ben waved her toward a chair before perching himself on the edge of his desk. "I asked you to come here tonight because I think we need to talk."

"About what?"

He'd chaired meetings with heads of state and heads of business, and never—even for a moment—had he felt at a loss for words. Now, with Kate looking up at him expectantly, he hadn't a clue how to begin.

He shoved his hands in his pockets and crossed his legs at the ankle. The pose was deliberately casual. "It's this arrangement we've made. It isn't working."

Kate's eyes widened, then she quickly averted her gaze. Damn, he was going to fire her. She should have known the situation was too good to last.

"I made a mistake," Ben continued. "And I'm willing to accept the blame."

"It wasn't your mistake." Kate stood. If it was over, then there was no reason to stay. "I never should have accepted your offer. I wasn't right for the job, but I was only thinking of myself, of what I needed, or maybe what I wanted—"

"Kate?"

She looked up. "Don't stop me now, I'm on a roll."

"Maybe." The corners of Ben's mouth curved upward. "But what are you doing?"

"Quitting." Kate snorted in exasperation. The least the man could do was have the decency not to look so pleased about it. "What does it sound like?"

In an instant, Ben's amusement vanished. "You're quitting your job?"

"What's the difference?" Kate glared at him. "You're about to fire me."

"No, I'm not."

"But you said—"

"I said that I'd made a mistake," Ben finished gently. "And I did. But it wasn't in hiring you to be my driver."

Kate's legs weakened, and she dropped back into the chair. "Then what was it?"

"You placed a condition on your acceptance of the job, and I agreed to abide by it. Remember?"

Slowly Kate nodded.

"I've changed my mind."

"What . . ." Kate cleared her throat and tried again. "What does that mean?"

Now that he was back in control, Ben began to feel more confident. "I want you, Kate. Hell, it's no secret. But I just didn't see how it could work. I thought . . ." He paused, raking a hand back through his hair. "I thought maybe if we saw enough of each other the attraction would wear off."

Kate leaned back in her chair and smothered a grin. "Ben?"

"Hmm?"

"You're a hopeless romantic."

He considered that for a moment. "Are you making fun of me?"

"Can I take the Fifth?"

So much for being in control. Ben pushed himself up from the desk and began to pace. "This isn't easy for me, Kate."

"I can see that."

He glowered. "It would be easier if you would stop laughing."

"I'm not laughing at you," Kate said honestly. "I'm laughing at both of us, at the situation. I mean, you have to admit, it's absurd."

"Of course, it's absurd," Ben grumbled. "And it's all your fault."

Kate schooled her features into some semblance of seriousness. "You mean the attraction didn't wear off?"

"No, it didn't wear off!"

"Good."

Ben stopped pacing and spun around. "What did you say?"

"I said 'Good.' Mine didn't wear off, either."

"At least that's something," Ben muttered. He'd never met anyone, man or woman, who was able to unnerve him the way Kate Hallaby did. And the fact that she did it so effortlessly only made things worse.

"So," Kate demanded, "now that we've gotten that out of the way, what are we going to do about it?"

Ben strode behind his desk and gazed down to where Kate sat. "I'm having a house party in Wilton this weekend. I'd like you to come."

"As your driver?"

"As my guest."

"No." Kate shook her head vehemently. "Out of the question."

"You asked me once before why I didn't just ask you out," Ben reminded quietly. "I'm doing it now."

"To a *house party?*"

"You know as well as anyone what my schedule is like. There isn't much spare time, even on the weekends. In my position, I have to do my share of entertaining. This party was arranged weeks ago. It'll be small. Only twelve people or so—"

"That's small?"

Ben ignored her interruption. "I want to see you, Kate. And not behind the wheel of that blasted Lincoln. I'm leaving for London on Sunday night— I'm sure Donald's filled you in. This is the best I can do."

"Well, it's not good enough." Kate sighed with frustration. "Surely you can see how awkward it would be. I'm your driver, Ben. I can't just show up on your arm."

Ben folded his arms over his chest with the conviction of a man used to making his own rules. "Why not?"

So help her, she was tempted. But that didn't mean she was crazy enough to agree. "When you get back—"

"This weekend," Ben stated implacably. She was lucky he wasn't insisting on tonight. He might have, too, if he hadn't thought she might need some time to get used to the idea. "You love the country. You told me so yourself."

He had her there. How many other things about her had he filed away for future use? "You don't do anything by half measures, do you?"

"When I want something," Ben said quietly, "I go after it."

The softly spoken words sent a tingle racing down the length of Kate's spine. Desire was there, but something else, as well: apprehension. Ben had a great deal of power over her life. All at once Kate needed to know how far he'd go to use it. "And if I refuse, then what?"

"I'll just have to change your mind, won't I?" Ben straightened, slipping one hand into the pocket of his pants. "How's your luck, Kate?"

She eyed him warily. "Just fine, thanks."

"I'll tell you what." He grinned. "I'll flip you for it."

Kate watched as he polished the dime on his shirt sleeve. "What do I get if I win?"

"How about a weekend in the country?"

Her laughter was low and easy. "Try again, hotshot."

Ben tumbled the dime, end over end, in his hand. "How about a raise?"

"You pay me too well now."

"Do I?" He shot her a look. "That can be remedied."

"Forget I mentioned it." Kate considered her options. Either way, she had little to lose. Either way, she ended up with . . . Ben. Suddenly feeling buoyant and more than a little reckless, she nodded toward the coin. "Go ahead, flip it."

Ben spun the dime high into the air. "You called it last time. This one's mine." He caught the coin in his palm and slapped it over onto his wrist. "I'll take heads."

Kate got up to look as he slowly lifted his hand. The coin was faceup.

"We'll leave Friday at two," Ben told her. "I'll pick you up at your apartment."

Kate nodded. Reaching around behind her, she picked up her hat. "Am I driving or do I have the weekend off?"

Ben looked up, surprised by the question. "You didn't need to ask that, Kate."

"Yes, I did."

Did she try his patience on purpose? Or did it simply come naturally? "We'll take the Jensen. *I'll* drive."

"All right. I'll be ready." She paused, her fingers swinging the cap by the brim. "I guess you won this round."

Ben stared at her across the room, and the look was as intimate as a lover's caress. Kate felt herself grow warm, heat flowing through her like melted honey. If that look was anything to go by, she was in for a wild ride.

"No," Ben murmured. "We both did."

"IT'S A GOOD THING we're the same size," said Maggie. "Otherwise you'd be up the creek."

"I probably will be anyway," Kate replied, looking at the pile of clothing—selected from both their wardrobes—spread out across the bed. "And what I'll be wearing has nothing to do with it. What do you think of my blue sweater?"

Maggie studied the garment critically. "Too innocent." She opened a drawer and yanked out another. "Here, take my red instead. Don't tell me you're having second thoughts already?"

"Not about Ben," said Kate. "But certainly about the weekend. What if there are people there who recognize me as his driver?"

"So what?" Maggie folded the red sweater and placed it in the suitcase.

"Don't you think that'll be a little strange?"

"I'm no judge," Maggie said wryly. "If you ask me, everything that's happened to you in the last month is strange. Including the fact that the high-and-mighty Benjamin West seems to have the hots for you."

"Don't worry," Kate said, deadpan. "He's hoping it'll wear off."

Maggie broke up in giggles. "Like the twenty-four hour flu?"

"Forty-eight," Kate corrected, and though she laughed as well, the thought of the weekend's span sobered them both.

Maggie picked up one of her lacy teddies and, ignoring Kate's look, stuffed it into the suitcase. "I just hope you know what you're doing. Not that you're not a great person, but a man like Benjamin West has his pick of the entire world. Don't go reading more into the situation than is there."

"I won't," Kate said. She closed the top of the suitcase and snapped the latches shut. "Ben's a wonderful man—probably the most incredible person I've ever met. I'd have to be crazy to think his interest in me was going to last forever."

She swung the suitcase off the bed and carried it over to the door. "But, so what? There's nothing I can do about that but ignore it. The way I see it, it's like being on a roller coaster. I know someday the ride's bound to end, but for now I'm just going to hang on and enjoy."

The downstairs buzzer sounded. Kate hurried into the bathroom for a last-minute check in the mirror, then grabbed up her suitcase and ran. Four flights later, she flung open the door to the vestibule—and strode right into Ben's arms.

His hands came up to steady her. Then he took the move one step further, folding his arms around her and pulling her to him for a warm, hard hug. Feeling giddy, Kate struggled to catch her breath. Four flights of stairs at top speed could do that to a person. Which also explained why she felt so wobbly when he let her go.

"When you change the rules," she observed, tilting her face up to his, "you don't fool around."

Ben's grin was amused—and sexy as hell. "Do you mind?" he countered, taking her suitcase, then opening the outer door.

"Not at all." Kate paused on the step. When Ben gestured toward a dark green sports car double-parked in the middle of the narrow street, she headed in that direction. "Actually, I think I like it."

Walking behind her, Ben warmed with pleasure. "You never lie to me, do you, Kate?" he said as he opened the trunk and stowed the suitcase inside.

"Not if I can help it." She leaned on the roof of the car, tapping a finger on the black canvas. "Does this thing go down?"

"Of course." Ben unlocked her door and handed her inside, before adding meaningfully, "When it's warm out."

"It's warm now."

He slid behind the wheel. "Says who?"

"Come on, this is the best day we've had in months."

"Considering those months were January, February and March, that's not saying much."

She tried a beguiling smile. "I'll bet it's sixty."

"Fifty," Ben corrected firmly, fitting the key into the ignition. "And you're pushing that."

"What's the matter?" Kate teased. Her hand slipped across the back of the bucket seats, fingers reaching upward. "Afraid you'll muss your hair?"

With a single, quick motion, Ben reached out and grabbed her hand, trapping it in his own. "You're determined, aren't you?"

"Very." She could feel his warmth seeping into her from the spot where their fingers were joined. It was like the tiniest of electrical currents, making her tingle all over. And still he didn't let go.

"And stubborn."

"That, too." Kate sighed. "Are you going to give me back my hand?"

"I'm considering it." He was also considering using it to haul her across the seat and into his arms.

"You'll need both hands to put the roof down."

Shaking his head, Ben released her. "Are we going to discuss this all the way out to Wilton?"

"That depends."

"Don't tell me. I may as well give in now, right?"

"Right." Kate reached for the latch on her side.

Resigned, Ben did the same. "If you get sick," he warned, "I'm docking your pay."

"Done." Kate smiled with delight as the roof lifted free above them. Tilting back her head, she closed her eyes and raised her face to the sun.

It was worth it, thought Ben, as he grabbed his suede jacket from the back seat and slipped it on. He'd never met a woman like Kate before—someone who could argue with conviction one minute, and sigh with the delight of a child, the next. There was an appealing intensity to the way she threw herself into life, and to her enjoyment of its most basic pleasures.

When he was with her, the way he approached life seemed to change. She reminded him of a part of himself he'd assumed he'd lost along the way. There were so many things he took for granted now; and so many things he hadn't the time to stop and enjoy. Somehow, in the single-minded struggle to achieve the goals he'd set for himself, he'd forgotten how simple life could be. And how sweet.

"Well?" Kate opened one eye and cocked her head in his direction. "What are we waiting for?"

"Nothing." Ben turned the key and the car started with a low rumble. They beat most of the traffic and were out of the city within minutes. The Jensen was at its best running full throttle, and once they reached the highway, he let it out.

Wind whipped through Kate's hair and slapped against her cheeks. She didn't mind in the least. Turning on the radio, she dialed quickly to a classic-rock station and turned the volume up. The steady, throbbing beat of the Rolling Stones filled the air. Smiling, Kate began to sing along.

Ben had driven the route often enough to know it well—a good thing, considering that he was having a hard time keeping his eyes on the road. When he'd run through the plans for this weekend in his mind, he'd pictured something entirely different.

With its top up, the Jensen was small enough to be cozy, even intimate. Ben had several classical tapes stored under the dashboard, and some pâté and crackers in a cooler behind the seat. The drive to Wilton was to have been warm and slow, easing them gently into the weekend to come.

Yet here he was, thought Ben, freezing his butt, pushing the speed limit and joining Kate in a chorus of "Jumping Jack Flash." Not only that—he wouldn't have changed a thing.

By the time they reached Connecticut, Kate was feeling thoroughly relaxed. Somehow in the course of the trip, her misgivings about the weekend had melted away. So what if she was spending the next two days with a dozen people with whom she had absolutely nothing in common? Ben would be there, and somehow, she'd find a way to make it work.

When a commercial came on the radio, she lowered the volume and turned to face him across the seat. Ben's cheeks were flushed from the cold, and his hair was rumpled just the way she liked it best. One hand held the steering wheel, the other rested lightly atop the gearshift. His fingers were long and slender, his nails buffed and blunt cut.

Strong hands, Kate observed. Not those of a laborer, but of a man who was accustomed to working for what he wanted, nonetheless. A man who drove with the confidence of someone who always knew exactly what he was doing. Just as he would know what he was doing when he put those hands on her. . . .

"So," said Ben, breaking into her thoughts. "How are you enjoying yourself so far?"

"Enormously." Kate smiled. "You can't imagine what a step up this is from public transportation."

"Oh, yes, I can." Ben glanced around. "By the way, did I tell you that the chairman of the Metropolitan Transportation Authority is going to be there this weekend?"

"The subway czar?"

"And his wife."

"Terrific." Kate gulped, then quickly recovered. "Who else among the rich and famous will I be wining and dining with?"

"Bibi and Calvin Latroux. They're clothing designers—"

"I know that." Kate frowned, considering. "I'll be underdressed."

"Don't worry about that—they'll be overdressed. They always are. Then there's Judge Aldous Warren and his wife."

"It's been rumored that he's going to resign the bench so he can run for the governorship next year," Kate commented.

"He is." Ben sent her a wink. "But you didn't hear it from me. I believe Al's bringing his aide. With any luck, the man will be entertained by Tabitha Bright."

"Bibi and Calvin's top model," Kate supplied.

"Right. Those are the only two on the list who aren't a couple. Hopefully, they'll manage to get along."

"From the pictures I've seen of Tabitha," said Kate, "there isn't a man in the world who couldn't cope."

She sank lower in her seat. She had to have been crazy to think she could pull this off. She'd be so far in over her head with this bunch, she'd be lucky if she didn't drown!

Watching out of the corner of his eye, Ben gauged Kate's reaction. If he didn't know better, he'd think she was intimidated. His Kate, who could get the better of a gun-wielding mugger, was suddenly speechless.

If there had been times in the past when he'd wished for just such silence, Ben knew now that they were a mistake. Observing her, he suddenly realized that Kate didn't turn such a tough face to the world because she cared so little, but because she cared too much. Beneath the hard outer shell was a soft and sensitive woman. A woman, Ben suspected, who had no idea just how incredibly alluring she really was.

A sign flashed by, announcing an exit. Ben made his decision. He put on his turn signal and eased into the right lane.

"What are you doing?" Kate asked as Ben pulled off the parkway. "That sign said Greenwich."

"Then I guess I'm going to Greenwich."

"I can see that." Kate looked around avidly as Ben headed down Round Hill Road. Huge mansions graced either side of the wide, tree-lined avenue.

"Do you mind taking a small detour?"

"No." Kate turned her head from side to side, trying to take it all in. "It's gorgeous."

Ben smiled to himself and kept on driving. When he reached the downtown area, he navigated with ease through the suburban traffic. Seeing an empty spot in the middle of Greenwich Avenue, he pulled the Jensen in and parked.

"Now what?" asked Kate.

"We stroll."

"What?"

"You know—walk, window-shop." Then, turning serious, Ben reached out and took Kate's hand in his.

"When we get to Wilton, everyone will be there. It won't exactly be a mob scene, but close. Maybe I'm being selfish, but I just wanted to have you all to myself for a little while longer."

Kate laced her fingers through Ben's and squeezed gently. She knew what he was doing. He'd seen the way she'd been thrown by his guest list, and he was giving her time to adjust. Ben wasn't a man who needed to defer to anyone. But now, though he had a houseful of guests waiting in Wilton, he cared enough to place her needs above his own.

Later, when Kate would think back to the moment that she first knew she was in love with Benjamin West, she would remember not a sudden flash of inspiration, but rather a warm feeling of peace that stole over her slowly. Right now, Kate knew she'd never been happier.

"All right?" asked Ben.

"Perfect." Kate looked up, her eyes shining. "Just perfect."

9

THE SUN WAS SHINING, the avenue uncrowded, and Ben was in a glorious mood. He grabbed Kate's hand and they strolled along the sidewalk, talking, laughing and browsing from one store window to the next. Kate sighed with delight over the lavish displays, as Ben leaned in and gazed over her shoulder, curious which items had made her smile.

"Why don't we go inside?" he suggested when she'd stopped for the third time.

"It's not necessary." Kate smiled up at him. "I'm perfectly happy out here."

"But you must have seen things you wanted."

"Sure, I have." Kate moved on from an expensive leather-goods store. "But that doesn't mean I'm going to buy any of them."

Ben considered that as Kate paused before a display of costume jewelry, intertwined with neon lighting. "Why not?"

"Why should I? These things are pretty, but I don't need them."

"We're not talking about what you need. What about what you want?"

Kate glanced up and shrugged. "It'll wait."

She hadn't sounded upset, Ben reflected, or even resigned. Merely philosophical, as if that was the way life was and she was used to it.

Another woman, surrounded by such bounty, would have been hinting like mad. Ben couldn't count the number of times one of his dates had just happened to take him by Cartier or Bulgari. Nor had he seen anything wrong with buying them the presents they all seemed to crave. It made them feel appreciated, perhaps even loved. And what was the matter with that?

But either Kate didn't know how such games were played, or else she wasn't interested in playing along. Perversely, Ben had never wanted to go on a shopping spree so much in his life as he did at this moment. Hell, what was money for, if not for making those you cared about, happy?

"I don't get it," he said.

Kate paused, waiting for him to catch up. "Get what?"

"I've never met a woman who didn't like spending money."

"And you call me a cynic."

"I'm not being cynical, merely realistic." Ben took her hand and led her to the next window, an expensive jewelry boutique. "Do you mean to tell me that if I offered to buy you anything you see, you wouldn't want a thing?"

"Well . . ." Kate looked around, then grinned mischievously. "There is one thing."

"Really?" Ben had expected to feel satisfaction, but not this unexpected burst of pleasure. Until that moment, he hadn't realized just how badly he wanted to treat Kate to something she couldn't afford to buy for herself, something special that would always remind her of this day and this time that they'd had together.

He gestured expansively toward the window. "Name it."

"There," Kate told him, pointing. Ben followed the line of her finger and found himself looking at the Häagen Dazs shop next door. "I want an ice-cream cone."

"That's it?"

Kate considered for a moment. "You could add sprinkles to the top."

He'd be damned if she wasn't serious, thought Ben. Right under her nose was a gold Rolex watch, and beside it, a sapphire the size of a ripe grape. Yet she'd passed them both by, and asked for ice cream. Nobody could be that innocent—least of all his tough-talking, streetwise Kate.

"You do realize what you're passing up?"

"Of course." Kate dismissed the jewelry display with a glance. "So what?"

"So I'm asking you why."

Deliberately Kate looked away. In the secluded grassy area beyond the shops was a bench beneath a tree whose leaves had just begun to bud. It was exactly what she needed. She snatched Ben's hand and dragged him toward it. "Sit!"

Ben considered arguing, then sat.

"I told you once before that you didn't have to pay me, and I meant it," she told him. "Whatever happens between us—this weekend or any other time—happens for one reason only. Because I want it to."

If she hadn't been so serious, Ben might have smiled. "Don't I have any say in the matter?"

"You do," Kate snapped, refusing to be sidetracked. "Your wallet doesn't. I can't be bought, Ben."

For a long moment he didn't say anything at all. Then he raised an arm to circle Kate's hip. Caught off balance, she tumbled into his lap. His other hand steadied her before both arms wrapped around her, holding her firmly in place.

"I never thought you could be," he said quietly.

"But—" Kate began, then stopped. It was impossible to maintain that edge to her anger when all her senses were on red alert.

She felt the hard muscles of Ben's thighs beneath her bottom. His shoulders tensed under her hands. His scent enticed her. His mouth drew her gaze. Moistening her lips, she tried to remember how to breathe.

"I'm sorry if I insulted you," Ben murmured. "I never meant to."

Kate opened her mouth but no sound came out. Ben's hand, resting on her hip, burrowed beneath her sweater. His fingers teased their way inside the waistband of her pants, grazing the smooth skin of her lower back. She shuddered at his touch, arching her spine into the caress.

Ben tilted her face to his.

"We can't," Kate breathed.

"I have to."

His lips closed over hers and Kate lost herself in the kiss. She who had always separated wanting and needing, found in that moment, that Ben could give her both. The kiss was long and insistent.

Desire, previously held in check, shivered through her. As she opened her mouth, Kate knew she'd never wanted anything as badly as she wanted Ben. The warmth of his body surrounded her. His taste sent her reeling. When his tongue plunged between her lips, Kate moaned at the delicious sensations radiating throughout her.

Ben wanted more, and he would have it—but not now, on a park bench in downtown Greenwich.

His hands came up, palms cradling the sides of her face as he gently pulled away. Kate's eyes were closed, her expression dreamy, and there was a soft sheen on her lips. And then she slowly smiled.

Yearning rocketed through Ben like a blow. Impulsively, he brushed his thumbs along the sides of her cheeks. When he took a deep, steadying breath, it didn't help.

Slowly Kate's eyes fluttered open. "That was nice."

"Nice, hell!" Ben picked her up and sat her beside him on the bench. "It was damn explosive."

"Maybe you shouldn't have waited so long."

"I was waiting," he said, "for you."

Kate lifted a brow at that.

"I was trying to take things slow," Ben growled. "Everything was changing between us. I thought you might need time to adjust."

"I see." Kate smiled then, and a mischievous light twinkled in her eyes. "Come on, let's go."

"Where?"

"First, you promised me an ice-cream cone." She stood, slipping her hand into his. "And after that, you can take me home and I'll show you just how well adjusted I really am."

THEY HADN'T FORGOTTEN that Ben had guests arriving. It was just that things had gone so well so far, that they fully expected fate to continue to oblige him. Perhaps they'd be the first ones there. Or maybe they could slip in unnoticed. After all, it was just past five by the time they arrived in Wilton; surely an extra hour could be found for continuing what they'd started on the park bench?

Unfortunately, that hope dissolved as soon as they reached the top of the driveway. A Mercedes-Benz sedan was idling near the front door. Behind it stood Parker, unloading a matched set of Louis Vuitton luggage from the trunk. Ben meant to drive right by, going around to the back where they could let themselves in, but Parker prevented them with a wave of his hand.

"I'm glad you're here, sir," he said when Ben had let the Jensen roll to a stop. "Donald Rubin has been trying to reach you all afternoon. He seemed to think it was quite urgent. I told him you were expected but hadn't yet arrived. Shall I go in now and put the call through?"

"No—" Ben sighed heavily "—I'll take care of it, thanks."

Nodding, Parker gathered the luggage and headed up the wide front steps. Kate watched him for the long moment it took to bring her emotions back under control. All afternoon, she'd been riding on a wave of euphoria. Now she came back down to earth with a thud.

Ben had gone out of his way to make her feel important. And he'd succeeded. So much so, that for a brief time she'd forgotten just how prominent a person he really was. He had other obligations and other commitments, not the least of which was a houseful of guests. She'd had him all to herself for several hours, and the time had been very special. But she had to have been crazy to think it could continue.

"I'm sorry." Ben thrust the Jensen into gear and drove around the side of the house. "Donald has a very long fuse. If he thinks something's urgent, then I really do have to call him back."

"That's all right. I understand."

"Do you?" Ben parked by the side of the driveway, then turned to face her across the seat. His hand, resting on the shift, slid across to her thigh and squeezed gently. "Then understand this. After I finish with Donald, I'll be greeting my guests. And the whole time I'm doing both those things, I'll be wishing I was upstairs alone with you. I'll be imagining the way you'll look when I slip those clothes from your delectable body. I'll be thinking about those sounds you make when we kiss, and how the pulse in your throat flutters beneath my fingers.

"I'll be shaking hands and mixing drinks and making small talk, and inside I'll be wondering whether you'll be shy or bold when we come together. Will you wrap those long lovely legs around me? Will the taste of you be spicy or sweet? I'll be wanting you in my arms, in my bed—" Ben gave a low, throaty growl "—and I'll be frustrated as all hell."

He leaned across the seat and kissed her hand. Then, just as quickly, he pulled back. "Come on, we'd better go in."

Kate swallowed heavily, staring after Ben as he got out and opened the trunk. Go inside? After that kiss, she was lucky she could even think, much less walk and talk.

Ben reappeared at her door. "Up you go," he told her, looking positively smug as he took her arm and helped her out of the car. "Parker will show you to your room. Take some time to freshen up, if you like, then come on down to the library. We'll be starting there with drinks before dinner."

No sooner had they entered the house, than Ben excused himself and went off to his study. Left in the front hall with her suitcases, Kate was relieved when Parker came bustling down the stairs to rescue her.

"Ah, Miss Hallaby. Good that you could make it."

"Thank you." Kate tried out a smile. It wasn't returned. No doubt Parker had seen dozens of women come and go, though probably none in such odd circumstances as hers. If he wasn't going to allude to their earlier meeting, however, neither was she.

"Shall we go up?" Parker asked, picking up her bag.

"By all means."

On her first visit to Ben's country house, Kate hadn't taken the luxury of looking around. Now, as Parker led the way up the broad, curving staircase to the second-story landing, she saw how truly grand a place it was. The hallway was a wide, sweeping corridor, furnished with tables and a settee. An alcove at the end held a wing chair. Fresh flowers were everywhere, their heady scent mixing with that of lemon wax.

Last time, Kate had been put in the bedroom at the top of the stairs. Now Parker led the way past two sets of doors and stopped at the third. The room was bright and cheerful, its color scheme cream and yellow, with accents of Wedgwood blue. Wide double windows looked out over the front meadow. They were open, their lacy curtains fluttering inward. The four-poster bed was made of brass, and its coverings were undeniably feminine. Gazing around, Kate smiled with delight. She felt like Cinderella and Alice in Wonderland, rolled into one.

"Shall I send someone up to help you unpack?" Parker asked primly.

"Don't bother—" Kate laughed "—I think I can handle it."

"Fine, then. I'll leave you. The bathroom's here. You'll be sharing it with Miss Bright, whose room is on the other side. Come downstairs whenever you're ready. The library's the last door on the left."

"Thank you," Kate said, turning around, but the houseman was already gone.

Quickly she unpacked her bag and hung up her clothes in the closet. That done, Kate pulled off the pants she'd traveled in and changed into a shimmering blue silk dress with a crossover bodice and flowing skirt. She added only a pair of earrings—wide, flat, silver disks, large enough to be seen among her chestnut curls.

Kate poked at her hair, then picked up her makeup bag and headed for the bathroom. The prospect of sharing with America's top model was daunting, to say the least; but when she knocked tentatively, then let herself in, the only sign of Tabitha's occupancy was a vast display of beauty products laid out along the counter.

"Sheesh!" Kate muttered, setting down the tiny bag that held her blusher, mascara and lipstick. "What is all that stuff, anyway?"

She examined several tubes, reading off labels with names like Nutramax, Skin Revival and Present Perfect. No wonder Tabitha looked so good. The woman probably spent a fortune on upkeep.

She reapplied her makeup, ran her fingers through her hair again, and was ready. Though it was obvious from the line of cars out front that people had been arriving all afternoon, she had yet to see anyone but Parker. The thought that she was about to meet a dozen of New York's most important people, en masse, made her stomach clench.

Ignoring it, Kate thrust back her shoulders and strode down the hall. By the time she reached the bottom of the stairs she could hear the hum of conversation coming from the direction of the library. She made her way to the open doorway, then paused for a look around.

The first person she saw was Tabitha, a tall blonde with the stunning looks of a Valkyrie, a knockout in ruby-red lamé. Beside her stood the jet-set publishing couple, Peter and Annette Rand. Judge Warren was there as well, as were Bibi and Calvin Latroux. Then Kate's gaze came to rest on Ben, and everyone else simply faded away.

He'd been talking to Bibi, but now he looked up. Their eyes met across the room, and the connection they made was strong enough to send a jolt all the way down to Kate's toes. Ben smiled in greeting, but his gaze was strangely intent.

Kate felt a rush of heat herself as his earlier words came flooding back.... *I'll be wanting you in my bed, in my arms.*

The spell was broken as Bibi Latroux's voice trilled out across the room: "Well, darling, I see *I've* lost your attention. And no wonder." She beckoned to Kate with the air of someone used to having her summons obeyed. "Don't stand in the doorway, dear. Come in. Ben, introduce us."

Bibi looked Kate over thoroughly as she approached. The inspection, though curious, was not unfriendly, and Kate felt herself begin to relax. Ben performed the introductions and poured Kate a drink. The four of them chatted for several minutes before Calvin excused himself to fill a plate with hors d'oeuvres. Then Bibi was hailed from across the room and Ben and Kate were left alone.

"You look lovely," said Ben, his voice low and husky. "Do you realize I've never seen you in a dress?" His gaze skimmed down to her legs and lingered for a long moment before slowly returning to her face. "If I'd known what I was missing, I think I'd have been tempted to have your uniforms redesigned."

"Don't," whispered Kate. Her cheeks were tinged with pink. "Don't you dare."

Ben's expression was deceptively innocent. "Dare what?"

"You know what I mean. Good Lord, you don't even have to touch me and I go all breathless and weak at the knees. Stop being so damn sexy, because so help me, Ben, if you turn me on right here, I'll . . ."

"Yes?"

It was only one word, but it was more than enough—the hairs on the back of Kate's neck began to stand up. "I won't be responsible for what happens," she warned.

"You intrigue me, Kate—" Ben smiled wolfishly "—as always."

"I'm not trying to intrigue you, dammit. I'm trying to threaten you."

"I'd never have guessed," Ben declared solemnly, but his words were belied by the twinkle in his eyes. "However, since you're the guest, I suppose I must respect your wishes. If you like, we'll change the subject."

"Good," Kate agreed.

"What would you like to discuss?"

"Anything," Kate said desperately. His dark eyes, though now trained on her face, were doing serious damage to her equilibrium. "Donald!" she cried with sudden inspiration. "Did you reach him?"

Ben sipped at his drink and nodded.

"And did you manage to solve your emergency?"

"For the time being." Reluctantly Ben shifted his eyes away from Kate's luscious and oh-so-tempting lips. "Remember the nightclub project I told you about a couple weeks ago? Now that the paperwork finally seems to have gone through, Mort Silverburg wants to break ground immediately. He told Donald that if I didn't have a crew down there by next week, he would."

"And that's a problem?"

"I'm not sure. That's why I'm not anxious to rush into anything. Anyway, I managed to get Mort on the phone and he's agreed to hold off at least another week—"

"You're monopolizing the lovely lady, Ben. Give the rest of us a chance."

Ben looked up into the round, jovial face of Judge Aldous Warren. "No way, Al. I know when I've got a good thing going."

"So does my Al." Maribeth Warren, a plump, smiling brunette, stood at her husband's side. "Never let it be said he missed the opportunity to meet a constituent."

"Al Warren," said the judge, offering his hand to Kate. "And this is Maribeth."

"Pleased to meet you," Kate murmured. Her hand was engulfed in a large, warm paw and pumped heartily.

"I don't believe you've met my aide," Judge Warren told Ben. "He's around here somewhere." He cast a glance about the room and found what he was looking for. "Barry, there you are. Come over here, son."

Kate caught a quick glimpse of blond hair glinting in the overhead lighting. Beneath that were lean shoulders, encased in a trim, Italian suit. She stiffened, almost imperceptibly, with shock. Then Barry Kingen turned around and Kate found herself face-to-face with her former lover.

As he crossed the room to join them, Kate noted that he still moved with the same lazy grace. A man on the way up. She hadn't seen him since January—not since the night he'd told her she wasn't good enough for him and walked out of her life. Four long months. It wasn't nearly long enough.

She'd put all that behind her. Or so she'd believed. But then, she'd never expected to see Barry again. Oh, God, thought Kate. Why here? Why now?

"Mr. West—" Barry extended his hand "—it's a pleasure."

Barry hadn't noticed her yet. Of course, she should have known that walking across the room he'd have seen only Ben. Barry had always been a man with his eye fixed firmly on the main chance.

Then Ben's arm was slipping around behind her waist, inching her forward for the introduction. "And this is—"

"Barry..." Kate broke in before Ben could go any further. Her smile felt as though it were made of plaster. "How nice to see you again."

She would always remember the first, fleeting expression on his face. Stunned, and just the tiniest bit outraged. Barry recovered quickly, however.

"Kate!" he cried. "What a wonderful surprise."

He leaned toward her, and it was all Kate could do not to angle away. Oddly enough, it was the warm pressure of Ben's arm at her back that held her steady as Barry kissed her cheek.

"Well, look at that." Judge Warren laughed. "Maybe you don't have the monopoly you thought you did, Ben."

Barry's brow furrowed all the way up into his hairline. Kate gritted her teeth in annoyance. How she could have ever found him attractive? Whatever she had once felt for Barry was now truly gone.

"Barry and I went to school together," she said for Ben's benefit. "But we haven't seen each other for a long time."

"I see." Ben looked back and forth between them. He recognized the name now. It had once meant enough for Kate to whisper it in her sleep. "Shall we leave you two alone to catch up?"

Kate started to reply, but Barry deftly cut her off.

"Not at all," he said smoothly. "Kate and I can reminisce later. But I would like to ask you your opinion on the mayor's proposed site for the new toxic-waste dump...."

Kate listened for only a moment before tuning him out. At least Barry was predictable. Clearly, when it came down to a choice between her company and Ben's, she wasn't even in the running. Not that she minded. The only problem was that now that Barry, ever ambitious, had Ben's attention, he wasn't about to give it up. When Kate finished her drink she drifted away, leaving the three men embroiled in a fervent discussion of New York's newest tax laws.

"It's terrible, isn't it?" Maribeth confided, following her to the bar. "They tell you it's going to be a fun weekend, and before you've even unpacked your bags, they're already talking shop."

Kate murmured assent and poured herself another martini. Actually, under other circumstances, she'd have thrown herself into the men's conversation with gusto. But not tonight, with Ben defending one side of the issue and Judge Warren supporting the other just as firmly, leaving Barry to bounce back and forth between them in a thinly veiled effort to please everybody. No, that was one discussion she was well out of.

Instead Kate picked up her drink, put on a smile, and mingled with the other guests. To her surprise, Bibi Latroux took her under her wing, calling her over and introducing her to the other couples whom she hadn't yet met. Half an hour later, when they went in to dinner, Kate found herself seated with Calvin on her left and Lawrence Smith-Miller, the architect, on her right. Both were interesting men and stimulating dinner companions, and went out of their way to see that she lacked for nothing.

Though Ben, seated at the head of the table, was busy entertaining his guests, it was obvious that Kate was never far from his thoughts. Several times she glanced up to find herself the object of his gaze, and the smoldering looks he trained in her direction were enough to make her squirm in her seat. Once, catching her eye, Ben dropped one lid in a broad, outrageous wink. Kate choked on a sip of wine and resolved firmly to look elsewhere. As for Barry, seated next to Tabitha and barely visible on the other side of the large, floral centerpiece, neither she nor Ben paid him any attention at all.

After dinner, brandy was served in the living room where a fire had been laid to ward off the early-spring chill. A curio cabinet offered up a large selection of games, but when Ben suggested Monopoly, he was roundly and jovially booed. Instead they chose sides and played charades, the highlight of the evening coming when Tabitha, who proved to be an apt and eager player, acted out her interpretation of *Cat on a Hot Tin Roof*.

By midnight, couples were beginning to head up to their rooms. Looking for Ben, Kate found him by the fireplace. He was leaning against the marble mantelpiece, deep in conversation with Peter Rand. Backlit by the glow from the dying embers, Ben looked warm and virile—and dangerously male.

There was a loud pop as a burning log fell from the andiron with a shower of sparks. When Ben glanced down, light flickered over the strong line of his jaw, and the shadowed hollow of his neck. Muscles shifted along his thigh as he lifted one foot to nudge the log back into the grate. With a hiss, the fire settled into place. Ben ignored it, reaching up instead to rake his fingers through his thick, springy hair. Peter laughed at something he said, and after a moment, Ben joined him.

Kate could have stood there watching all night. There was nothing about Benjamin West that she didn't find fascinating. And though she wanted him with her, she could wait. For now, just the anticipation of having him all to herself later was enough.

Even as that thought crossed her mind, Ben looked up. His eyes met Kate's and he smiled. A moment later, he excused himself and came over.

"I need a few more minutes with Peter. Do you mind going up alone?"

Suddenly feeling shy, Kate shook her head.

"I won't be long." Ben brushed a soft kiss across her lips. "Promise."

"Do you, um . . . know which room I'm in?"

Ben's dark eyes gleamed. "Ah, sweet Kate, you underestimate me."

The husky undertone of his voice, the naked desire in his gaze, made Kate shiver. "I just didn't want you getting lost, that's all."

"Not a chance," Ben whispered, his lips only inches from her ear. "I'm right across the hall."

Kate chuckled softly. "I guess it pays to have connections."

"Always."

A throat cleared behind them and Kate looked up. Aside from Peter, they were the only ones left in the room. She could hardly begrudge him a few more minutes when the art of wheeling and dealing was so intrinsic to the nature of this man she'd come to love.

"Go on," she said. "Finish your talk. And when you do, I'll be waiting."

She felt his eyes upon her as she crossed the room. Then she turned the corner and ran up the stairs with a smile.

10

Up in her room, Kate did the only thing she could think of: She got ready for bed. The nightgown she'd brought with her was the most seductive piece of clothing she owned—a shimmering sweep of ecru satin, with a low, lace-draped bodice and tiny spaghetti straps. Now, sliding it on over her bare skin, Kate shivered with anticipation. There was a matching peignoir and she slipped that on as well, leaving its satin ties free.

One by one, she flicked off the lights until the only illumination in the room was a strip of silvery moonlight, falling across the floor. She'd just pulled back the coverlet on the bed when the knock came.

Tremulously, Kate answered, "Come in," and started forward as the door opened. She stopped midstride, the smile fading from her lips.

"Well, well, well." Barry looked around and grinned. "This is some reception."

Startled into silence, Kate could only stare as he reached back with one foot and nudged the door shut. "Waiting for me, were you, Kate?"

She didn't know which was worse—the question or the leer that went with it. "Certainly not," Kate snapped, reaching for the ties of her peignoir and lacing them up tightly. "What are you doing here?"

"I think you know." Barry took a step forward, and then another, until his hands reached up to her shoulders. "There's always been chemistry between us, Kate. I think there still is."

Deftly she eluded his grasp, flicking on the lamp on the night table as she scooted to the other side of the bed. "You're wrong, Barry. Whatever we once had is long gone."

"I've missed you, Kate," he said earnestly.

"I could tell. It was the constant calls and letters that tipped me off." Striding past the dresser, Kate switched on the light there, as well.

"I've been busy."

"I'll bet you have." She reached the door and opened it. "Now go be busy elsewhere."

"You're looking great, Kate."

"Thank you." She gestured toward the open doorway.

Blindly determined, Barry ignored the invitation to leave. "We made a connection downstairs this evening. I felt it. You can't tell me you didn't feel something, too."

Of course she had, thought Kate. Her emotions had run the gamut from shock to dismay.

"You must have known I'd come," he persisted. "You were waiting for me, Kate, weren't you?"

She didn't remember Barry being particularly stubborn, but he certainly wasn't getting the hint now. Would she be forced to shove him out of the room? "For the last time, get this into your head. I am not interested in you."

"Then who . . . ?" He slowly turned to look at her as comprehension dawned. "My, my. You certainly have landed on your feet, haven't you?"

"Come on, Barry!" Kate said impatiently. "Out!"

Now that he'd put it together, though, he wasn't ready to go quite yet. "I have to admit when I first saw you downstairs, I wondered what you were doing here. But then you always were the resourceful sort. I just figured you'd gotten Mr. West roped into supporting one of your lamebrained legal-aid projects—"

"I drive his car," Kate broke in. Anything to get him out of there. "That's our connection. I'm Ben's chauffeur."

"Sure." Barry laughed. "Right."

"Believe it or not, as you wish. I haven't got time to argue and, quite frankly, I couldn't care what you think, just as long as you do it in your own room."

"All right," Barry conceded, frowning. "I guess I can take a hint."

Especially when it hit him over the head with sledgehammer force, Kate thought irritably. No sooner was he through the doorway than she pushed the door shut behind him. Of all the nerve! Barry had always had an extremely high opinion of himself. Even so, his assumption that she might welcome him into her bed after he'd dumped her so callously made her blood boil. Lucky for him that she'd been in such a good mood when he arrived. Otherwise she might have been tempted to—

A knock came again: two quick, soft taps, just as before. Obviously Barry's ego was not about to allow him to accept defeat graciously. Hopping up off the bed, Kate strode across the room and threw open the door.

"Now what?" she demanded.

Standing in the hallway, Ben cocked an eyebrow at the bundle of fury standing before him. "Nothing like a gracious greeting to get things off on the right foot."

He started into the room, then hesitated. "Unless you'd rather I hadn't come?"

"No, of course not." Kate took Ben's arm and led him forward, then shut the door behind him. "I'm sorry, I didn't mean to yell. I thought you were someone else."

"Really?" Ben cleared his throat, sounding not at all pleased. "Who?"

"Oh, for Pete's sake," Kate muttered. Her romantic plans were in shambles. She was flushed and furious. The room was lit up brighter than a Christmas tree and her peignoir was laced up as if it were guarding Fort Knox. And now she had Barry to explain, as well.

"Barry Kingen just stopped in for a minute, that's all."

"Your old friend."

It was as much a question as a statement. Kate settled for a nod.

"Looking to renew your acquaintance?"

"He was. I wasn't."

"I gathered that from the greeting I got," Ben said dryly. He'd never met a woman more capable of fending for herself than Kate, but that didn't stop him from asking, "Do you want me to send him home?"

Kate looked up, imagining the furor such a move would cause. "No . . . of course not."

"If the man was bothering you—"

"He wasn't," Kate replied firmly. "Believe me, nothing Barry could say or do makes the slightest difference to me."

"I see." Ben swung his gaze around the room. "Got the place pretty well lit up, haven't you?"

Kate gave him a look. "Don't you dare laugh at me."

"Be glad I'm laughing." Ben's tone was deceptively mild. "Otherwise I might be tempted to find Kingen and throttle him." He slipped out of his jacket and tossed it over the back of a chair. "There's just one thing that stops me."

Kate's breath caught. "What's that?"

He took two steps and walked her straight into his arms. His body was warm and wonderfully solid. Kate molded herself against it and inhaled sharply, drinking in his scent. Ben's hand came up to tangle in her hair.

"Don't you know?" he asked softly.

Kate lifted her face to his. "Tell me."

"The sight of you, dressed like that." Ben sighed with a sound that came from deep in his throat. "I've been waiting for this moment for days, weeks, forever. I've thought about it, dreamed about it, taken it to a dozen cold showers. I wouldn't care if the house was on fire, sweet Kate. I couldn't leave you now."

"Then stay," Kate whispered, emotion shining in her eyes. "And love me, Ben."

Slowly he lowered his lips to cover hers in a kiss that was as gentle as the sweetest of dreams. There was fire burning inside him, but for Kate's sake, Ben tamped it down. She was far too accustomed to making do. For once, he wanted her to have it all—soft whispers, tenderness . . . and sweet seduction.

Kate rose on her toes to return Ben's kiss. His hands rested, warm and heavy, on her hips. The feel of their weight excited her, the imprint of his palms seared her flesh. She angled her head and opened her mouth. Ben's tongue slipped between her parted lips.

He moaned and Kate quivered at the sound. Her breasts swelled, lifting the filmy lace. Sinuously, she moved back and forth against his chest. Ben drew her forward so that their hips ground together.

His eyes were closed, his breath rasping. "I wanted this to be slow and easy."

"Hmm," Kate murmured, trailing a line of kisses along his jaw. "I was aiming for fast and hard."

Ben felt his stomach muscles clench. He'd never met a woman who excited him as she did, nor one he wanted more to please. "You deserve the best, sweet Kate. Romance, tenderness . . ."

Her hands lifted to Ben's tie. She unknotted it and tossed it away. "I have the best," Kate whispered, looking up into his eyes. "I have you."

With a groan, Ben brought his mouth down on hers in a kiss that was almost rough. There was no middle ground to the way he felt about Kate. Take away the barriers he'd erected between them, and raw passion rushed in.

He'd experienced it each time they'd kissed. He'd known that she was one woman who could carry him to the limits of control and beyond. Ben knew, right then, that there would never be an end. No matter how much he had of her, it could never be enough.

Kate unfastened the buttons on Ben's shirt and slipped it off. She stroked his shoulders, his arms. His flesh was sleek and hot beneath her fingers as she explored his chest, then lingered in his dark, springy mat of hair. She wanted to feel all of him—hard and naked—against her without the barrier of clothing between them.

Kate's hands moved to the ties on the front of her peignoir. Then all at once they stilled, as Ben covered them with his own. "No," he murmured against her mouth. "Let me."

One by one, he pulled the bows free. Kate trembled as his hands slipped beneath the robe and eased it from her shoulders.

For a long moment, Ben didn't move at all. But though he did nothing but look, it was more than enough. Kate shuddered at his hungry gaze. She was throbbing in anticipation of what was to come.

With his hands resting on her shoulders, Ben slid a thumb beneath each silken strap. His palms shifted as his thumbs gently drew the straps downward to the upper edge of the bodice. Kate's breasts ached for his touch. Instead, his hands lifted, retracing their path upward as he raised the straps and gently eased them off her shoulders.

The gown slipped down several inches, then held. Kate lost her breath as Ben lowered his head to kiss the curve of her breasts. His hands framed her waist, then moved up over her rib cage as his lips grazed their soft skin again and again. His heart was pounding when his tongue found the hard point of her nipple, still encased in lace.

Kate gasped as he drew the nipple into his mouth. The wet heat of his tongue brushing over the lace created a delicious friction that was almost more than she could bear. Ben muttered something under his breath. She couldn't make out the words but it didn't matter— the sound alone was enough to make her head spin.

He lifted his head and as he did, the gown lost its hold and slipped away. "Sweet Kate," Ben murmured. He swept her up into his arms and carried her the few feet to the bed where he gently laid her down on the cool sheets. "Sweet, beautiful Kate."

Now it was her turn to watch Ben as he stripped away the rest of his clothes.

Earlier, she'd wanted the room in darkness and shadow, but now she was glad the lights blazed so that her gaze could roam intimately over every incredible inch. Beneath the British suits and the starched shirts lay the lean, muscular frame of a primitive warrior. Her warrior. Her man.

Kate held out a hand and the bed dipped as Ben climbed in beside her. They came together in a kiss, but it wasn't nearly enough. Their hands were moving, touching, feeling, and still it wasn't enough. Ben rolled Kate over so she was beneath him, his weight solid and heavy as he held her in place.

Her chestnut hair fanned out over the pillow. Her lips were moist, her blue eyes dark with desire. He'd imagined this moment a hundred times. He'd known making love with her would be glorious; what he hadn't expected was this need to protect as well as pleasure her. He wasn't the type for making promises. Yet with Kate, Ben found himself wishing he was.

Instead he kissed her deeply and gave himself over to the sensation. As she responded in kind, his hand covered her breast and he felt her heart racing. He couldn't get enough, he couldn't give enough.

"Ben," Kate whispered as he lifted his head. "I forgot..."

"That's all right." He shifted his weight, reaching for the foil packet in his pants. "I didn't."

As he entered her moments later, Kate felt pleasure, desire, and love in a combination so potent she thought she might burst. Then Ben began to move inside her and Kate was pulsing all over. She clung to him wildly, riding the wave to its crest. She cried out in her ecstasy, and he covered her mouth with his, as his body reached the powerful climax.

For a long time afterward, they both lay spent. The house around them was dark and quiet. As their bodies slowly relaxed, Ben reached behind them and found the quilt, flipping it up over them. Still he did not leave her.

There were a million things Kate wanted to say but found she couldn't utter any of them. Filled with love, she didn't dare speak the word aloud. She had only to listen to Ben's labored breathing to know that he was fulfilled, too. They'd shared something special, something rare. Kate wondered if Ben knew how truly lucky they were.

He looked at her. "Any minute now, I'm going to come back down to earth." He smiled whimsically. "Then again, maybe not."

"Good." Kate ran her hands down his back, palms skimming over the sweat-soaked muscles. "I'm glad I'm not the only one who feels as though she's floating in the clouds."

Ben raised himself up on his elbows. "Am I too heavy?"

"No." Kate set her hands on his shoulders so he couldn't go any farther. "You're just right."

Ben's smiled widened. "My sentiments exactly."

He'd given her so much, Kate reflected. And he'd done so without reservation. He'd offered her security, tenderness and caring. And what had she given him in return?

Her love, she knew, warming with the emotion. But not her honesty. She'd held back, and she'd done so on purpose. Kate realized how wrong she'd been. They'd shared their bodies. Someday, they'd share their souls. Now was the time for a tentative beginning. And if he wasn't ready for a declaration of love, then she'd offer him what she could: her trust.

"Ben?" she murmured.

"Hmm?"

"There's something I've never told you."

"There are a lot of things you've never told me." Ben leaned on one elbow, to look into her eyes. "Your favorite color, for one. Your favorite food, for another. Are you a night owl by choice or necessity?" His mouth swooped down to plant a teasing nip in the hollow of her throat. Kate flinched, and he grinned at her response. "And I'm quite sure you never mentioned that your neck was ticklish."

Delighted by his mood, she played along. "Blue, nacho chips and necessity. As for being ticklish, I take the Fifth."

"I don't believe you," Ben said firmly. "Nobody's favorite food is nacho chips."

"Mine is."

"Next you'll be telling me you like Twinkies."

"I do."

"Good Lord—" Ben groaned "—what have I gotten myself into?"

"Too late for second thoughts now."

Ben's hand moved to her breast and stroked gently. The brush of his thumb across her nipple made Kate's back arch. "But not," he qualified, "for thoughts about seconds."

"You're terrible."

Ben leered at her teasingly. "Tell me again in five minutes."

"In five minutes, I'll be beyond speech."

"No problem." Ben smiled. "So will I."

"You are," Kate drawled, "the most distracting man I've ever met." She placed her hand over his, then waited until he looked up into her eyes. "I'm trying to tell you something."

"So am I."

Laughing in spite of herself, Kate pressed on. "There's something I want you to know. I wasn't always a cabbie, or a saleswoman in a boutique. Before I dropped out last January, I was a third-year law student at NYU."

Ben waited a beat, then said quietly, "I know."

"What?"

"For security reasons, a background check is always run on anyone who's going to be working closely with me." Ben shrugged, almost apologetically. "It came up in the report."

She'd meant to surprise him. Instead she was the one taken aback. "Why didn't you tell me?"

"I was waiting for you to tell me. I figured there had to be a reason why you didn't."

Kate bit her lip.

"Well?" Ben prodded.

"I wanted you to like me for myself," Kate explained slowly. "No matter who I was, or what I did, I didn't want it to matter to you."

"It didn't." Ben's palm came up alongside her cheek, holding her steady for a long, slow kiss. "If anything, I was more intrigued than ever."

"You find me intriguing?"

"Very." This time when his mouth traveled down her throat, she didn't move. "Also infuriating."

"Really?" She could feel the excitement beginning all over again, the tension coiling inside her.

"Umm." His tongue curled around her nipple. His breath was warm and moist on her breast. "Have I ever mentioned that I hate snowdrifts?"

"Not till now." Kate smiled. "Shall I apologize for making you cold?"

"Make it up to me instead," Ben told her in a low, husky voice.

"How?"

"Make me hot."

She didn't need a second invitation.

KATE AWOKE to an empty bed and a feeling of delicious contentment. She had a hazy memory of Ben slipping out of the room just before dawn, then returning almost immediately to kiss her one last time before letting himself out again.

"See you at breakfast, sweet Kate," he'd whispered. Kate had smiled dreamily and drifted off to sleep once more. When she awoke again, it was eight o'clock.

She'd promised herself there'd be no regrets or recriminations, and there wouldn't be. There was no point to wondering what it would be like to waken in this house, in this bed, and know that she belonged there—not just for one night, but forever. Why waste her time wishing for what couldn't be?

She didn't believe in fairy tales or knights on white chargers, either. Daydreams were fine, but in the end, determination and hard work were what truly counted. This weekend was special and bore no relation to her real life. She'd deal with tomorrow when it came. But for now, she was going to make the most of what she had.

She took a long, hot shower, then dressed in a pair of gray corduroy pants and a hand-knit pullover.

Downstairs, she followed the smell of fresh coffee and crisp bacon to the breakfast room, a sunny alcove behind the kitchen whose large window overlooked the yard and the woods beyond. A breakfast buffet had been set up on the sideboard, and though the round oak table was set for six, only one chair was occupied.

Annette Rand, a slender, elegant blonde with high cheekbones and piercing green eyes, was drinking a cup of tea and scanning the morning paper. She looked up as Kate entered the room and pushed the *Times* aside. "Thank God, someone to talk to. Pop your head in the kitchen and Parker will fry you some eggs if you like. In the meantime, grab some coffee and come join me."

Kate filled a cup with the hot, fragrant Colombian brew, then piled a plate with two gooey cinnamon rolls. "Where is everybody?"

"Would you believe the men got up early and went off to play golf?" Annette rolled her eyes. "Bibi and Maribeth have gone for a walk. As for Tabitha, she's sleeping."

Kate slid into the chair beside her.

"Lord," said Annette, eyeing the selection on Kate's plate. "I must say I envy you that. Must be your age. Before I was thirty, I could eat anything." She laughed self-deprecatingly. "Now it's all herbal tea and oat bran."

Kate broke off a piece of the roll and slathered butter on it. "I'm just lucky. I've never had a weight problem."

"I can see that." Annette remarked with a sigh. Then she looked up at Kate. "We didn't have much of a chance to talk last night, but Peter said Ben was absolutely smitten. You must tell me everything."

Kate choked loudly on a bite of roll.

"I guess I'm being too forward. Well, don't let it bother you. I usually am."

"No bother." Kate gulped, clearing her throat.

"It's just that we all seem to run in such a tight little group that when a fresh face pops up, we're thrilled to have something new to talk about."

Kate blushed.

"Oh, dear." Annette eyed her distress. "I just assumed you'd know we were talking about you. To tell the truth, Bibi and I thought that Ben was absolutely adorable. I've never seen him act that way. Why, he never took his eyes off you all evening."

Kate hadn't the slightest idea what to say. Judging by the direction of the conversation so far, no doubt comments on Ben's after-hours visit would come next.

"So . . ." Annette dabbed at her lips with her napkin, then set it aside. "We'll start at the beginning. Tell me how you and Ben met."

Here it came—the moment she'd been dreading ever since Ben had asked her to join him for the weekend. It was only a matter of time before somebody was curious and her secret came out. Well, this was the time.

She could lie. She'd always been good at concocting stories and certainly, in this situation, a small white lie would go a long way toward smoothing things along. But almost as soon as she'd considered the possibility, Kate rejected it. She wasn't ashamed of who she was, and neither was Ben. He'd told her so himself. Compared to his approval, how much could Annette's opinion matter?

"We met in New York," Kate began.

"Well, of course." Annette poured herself another cup of tea. "Where else?"

"Ben flagged down a cab."

"How romantic! You were riding in it?"

"No," Kate said slowly. "I was driving it."

"You're a cabbie?"

"I was. Now I work for Ben. I'm his driver."

A long moment passed—a moment during which Kate deliberately busied herself with adjusting the amount of sugar in her coffee. Then she heard the silvery tinkle of Annette's well-bred laugh.

"Why, my dear, I think that's wonderful."

Kate looked up. "You do?"

"Unless I miss my guess, the indomitable Benjamin West has met his match."

Kate broke off another piece of roll. "Why do you say that?"

"Now, don't take this wrong," warned Annette, leaning closer. "I've known Ben for years. Of course he's dated his share of women, maybe more than his share— all beautiful, accomplished women. But it's been easy to see that he's been bored to death."

Kate sat back in her chair, wondering whether or not she'd just been insulted. "So you think he's ready for someone who isn't beautiful and accomplished?"

"That isn't what I meant at all! Of course you're every bit as lovely as his other women, but at the same time, you're different somehow."

There was something about Annette's honesty that made Kate want to lay all her cards on the table. "I'm poor," she stated bluntly. "That's the difference."

"I doubt if Ben gives it any thought."

"Aren't you the same person who just told me what a tight group it is that you all run in? I'm not part of society," Kate said firmly. "And I never will be."

"Don't be too sure of that." Annette's expression was positively smug. "Good God, child, do you think we were all to the manner born? Before I met Peter, I was a hairdresser."

Kate sat up straight. "You were?"

"I most certainly was. And a damn good one, too."

"But you look so . . . so . . ."

"Polished?" Annette prompted.

"Exactly."

"But my dear, fifty million dollars can do that to a person. Good God, I've been lifted, tucked, coiffed and dressed to within an inch of my life. How could I possibly go wrong?"

Kate smiled, liking Annette more and more by the minute. "And Peter didn't mind that you were a hairdresser?"

"Oh, I'd be willing to bet it gave him a moment's pause at the time. But in the end it came down to the fact that he wanted me." Annette nodded. "And he still does. So what difference does the rest of it really make?"

"In your case," Kate answered slowly, "none."

"Not only my case. Society's full of women who have pulled themselves up by their boot straps. Don't ever think that it isn't. Why, Maribeth started out as a schoolteacher. And Bibi?" Annette paused for a teasing wink. "Well, let's just say that we don't talk about what Bibi did before she met Cal, unless we're feeling particularly naughty."

At that moment Tabitha walked in, looking sleepy and more beautiful than anyone had a right to be. The conversation shifted to other topics, and as Rachel Smith-Miller came down and Bibi and Maribeth returned from their walk, the room filled up and Kate was able to slip away unnoticed.

It wasn't that she didn't like the other women, she realized as she pulled on a jacket and let herself outside, or that she didn't enjoy their company. No, quite the opposite was true. But for now, for a few minutes, she needed to be alone.

Alone with her thoughts. Alone with her dreams. Alone with the possibility that sometimes fairy tales might come true, after all.

11

THE REST OF THE WEEKEND passed too quickly.

Though the house was filled with people and activity, Ben and Kate managed to spend nearly all their time together. As host, certain duties were required of Ben, but whenever possible, he made sure that Kate was by his side. And though nothing was said aloud, Kate had the other women's support and approval. It was obvious in the way each took care to ensure that her husband didn't monopolize too much of Ben's time. As for Barry, to Kate's relief he'd given up on her and had managed to make do nicely with Tabitha Bright.

Saturday night, there was a small dinner dance, and Kate was glad she'd raided Maggie's wardrobe to supplement her own. The dress she wore was a midnight-blue sheath. Made of wool jersey, it fastened over one shoulder and left the other bare. Kate twisted her hair up into a chignon, then added a pair of small pearl earrings as the finishing touch.

Ready to go down, she opened the door only to find Ben standing there, his hand raised to knock. His arm fell to his side as he slowly looked her up and down. Then he gave her a wolf whistle.

"I guess I'll do," said Kate, glowing beneath his regard.

"Lady, you'll more than do. You'll make me very proud." Before Kate could say a word, Ben gathered her into his arms for a kiss that was warm and tender, and ended far too soon. "We'd better go down," he told her. "Much as I'm tempted to keep you all to myself, I can hardly deny my other guests the pleasure of your company."

Buoyed by his high opinion of her, Kate floated down the stairs. In addition to the guests who were staying at the house, another dozen had been invited for the evening. Ben had eyes only for Kate. He laced his hand through hers and kept it there, bringing her drinks, feeding her hors d'oeuvres and including her in his many conversations. After dinner, they danced the first dance together, and most of those that followed. Thoroughly absorbed in each other, they waltzed away the night and when, finally, the last of the guests had departed, Ben waltzed her upstairs to bed.

If their lovemaking the night before had been fast and fiery, tonight it was slow and tender—a celebration of their mutual enjoyment.

As Ben held Kate in his arms, his tongue explored the shell of her ear, the hollow of her throat. In movements that were languid and infinitely erotic, he continued to woo her with his mouth and hands.

Kate grew dizzy, lost in a haze of sensual enjoyment. The heat of arousal built within her until she was flushed and aching. Every place Ben touched, her body came alive as though it had been waiting only for this moment and this man.

Lifting her hands, Kate unfastened Ben's bow tie and tossed it aside. The studs on the front of his tuxedo shirt presented more of a challenge; she bent down before him to devote her full attention to the task.

"Let me help," Ben murmured, but Kate nudged his hands away.

"My turn." Given a gentle push backward, Ben sat down on the bed. Kate spread his thighs and knelt between them. She smiled up at him, her eyes gleaming. "I'm sure I'll get the hang of it eventually."

Ben moaned as her fingers unfastened the first stud and she parted the shirt and pressed her lips to his hot flesh. Her breasts pressed against his abdomen, and a spasm of desire shuddered through him.

"Eventually," Ben growled, "may not be soon enough."

Kate kept going. She unhooked the second stud, and then the third. Exposing the dark, curly hair of his chest, she leaned forward and kissed his breastbone, slowly rubbing her face back and forth, and reveling in the play of textures upon her skin.

"Kate..."

"Mmm?"

"You...are...making...me...crazy...."

"Good," Kate murmured as the fourth stud popped. She slipped both hands inside Ben's shirt and ran her thumbs over the nubs of his nipples. She heard Ben's breath catch.

"Enough."

"But I wasn't finished."

"Yes, you were."

Ben tossed his shirt aside. He rose to his feet, pulling Kate up with him. He held her until he was sure she was steady, then his hands went to the small knot at her shoulder.

"What happens if I undo this?"

Kate moistened her lips. "Try it and see."

The knot came loose and the dress slithered to the floor. Kate stood before him, clad only in a sheer strapless bra and silk panties.

Ben thought he'd never seen anyone so lovely, so incredibly enticing. His gaze never left her as he stripped off the rest of his clothes.

Ben took Kate in his arms and they tumbled to the bed together. He unhooked her bra and, tossing it aside, sucked her taut nipple.

"Make me yours," she pleaded.

"I will, sweet Kate. I will," he whispered as he filled her.

He began to thrust rhythmically, and Kate wrapped her legs around his hips as she responded to the exciting friction.

Deeply aroused by their frantic pace, they both cried out when the ecstatic release shattered their bodies and souls.

BY LATE AFTERNOON Sunday, the last of the guests had departed and only Ben and Kate were left. They stood in the doorway, waving, as Calvin and Bibi's Mercedes drove off down the drive. When it was gone, Ben leered at Kate teasingly. "Alone at last, my sweet."

Behind them, Parker discreetly cleared his throat. "I've packed your bags, sir. Need I remind you your plane leaves at six?"

Ben turned. The hand that had circled Kate's waist fell to his side. "No," he said, sighing. "You needn't remind me."

"Six?" Kate looked up. "For an international flight, that doesn't give you much time. Let me just get my bag and we can go."

"We?" Ben reached out to stop her, but she was already heading for the stairs. "We who?"

Kate paused, glancing back. "You and me. How else do you think you're getting to the airport?"

"Parker will take me."

"He will not. I'm your driver, remember?"

For just the briefest moment, Ben looked so genuinely startled that Kate wondered if it was possible that he'd forgotten that she was also his employee. They hadn't overcome any of their differences this weekend—merely set them aside. The past forty-eight hours had been a dream. Now it was time to wake up and go on.

They stowed their gear in the back of the Jensen and Ben slid behind the wheel. "If you want me to drive—" Kate began.

"I don't."

Well, that put her in her place. And if that hadn't, the hour-long drive out to Kennedy airport completed the job. Ben was silent, concentrating on the traffic and paying only the slightest attention to her feeble attempts at conversation. Mile by mile, Kate's mood darkened.

She slammed the car door loudly as she climbed out at the unloading zone at Kennedy. Why should he bother to be charming or even polite, for that matter? After all, she was only the hired help.

Removing his bags from the trunk, Ben looked up. "I know how you feel."

Kate glared at him. "I doubt that."

"You're angry."

"You bet I am."

He'd made a mistake. He should have confronted her at home—the very moment she'd made that crack about being his driver. He thought they'd managed to put all that behind them and that the weekend had shown her how much more they could have. He'd gained so much in the past two days. Was he about to lose it all now?

"I'm sorry." Ben hefted his suitcase onto the curb. "I don't want to go, either. Not now... Especially not now." His look sent heat flooding up into her cheeks. "But I've spent the last hour trying to think of some way to work around this trip, and I can't. I'd considered taking you with me, but I'm going to be working virtually nonstop. It'll only be five days." Ben frowned. "If it's any consolation, they'll be the longest five days of my life."

The more he said, the worse Kate felt. It wasn't the first time she'd misjudged Ben. But now she vowed it would be the last. He reached out his hand, and Kate grasped it as he pulled her up onto the curb beside him. Horns blared, traffic swirled around them. They saw only each other.

Ben's hand came up to frame her face. "Tell me you'll miss me."

"I'll miss you."

He kissed her until she trembled, and then he kissed her some more. "Five days," he repeated, as the skycap took his bag and tagged it.

"I'll be waiting."

Then he disappeared into the crowd of passengers heading into the terminal and was gone.

SINCE BEN WAS AWAY, Kate had the week off. There were a million things to see and do in New York—everything from plays, to art exhibits, to first-run movies. Now that she had the time and extra money, she planned a schedule that included as many as possible. Her days were filled from morning till night. She should have been having the time of her life—never had she been more miserable.

Two months earlier, had she found herself in this position—on paid vacation, with nobody to please but herself—she'd have thought she had it made. Now her days stretched before her, filled, and yet at the same time, unbearably empty. Was this a preview of what her life would be like when Ben was gone?

She hadn't wanted to think about that, but she knew she had to. Although Ben had shown by his actions that he cared for her, Kate now realized that that wasn't enough.

She wanted more. She wanted all the things that Ben had never mentioned and she had never asked for—love, respect and commitment. She wanted him to think of their relationship as more than a game whose outcome could be wagered on the toss of a coin.

She wanted too much. And that was nothing new. But this time there was a difference, because the tools she'd relied on in the past—guts, perseverance and sheer determination—were all useless now.

She could only hope, because this time it was all up to Ben.

BEN CALLED Thursday evening.

Robe on, feet up, Kate was preparing to spend the night with steamed dumplings, Moo Shoo pork, and a rerun of *Casablanca*, when the telephone rang.

"How's London?" she asked.

"Wet. How about New York?"

If she was going to go for it, she might as well go for broke. "Lonely."

"Really?" Ben sounded pleased. "It's only twenty-four more hours. That's what I wanted to talk to you about."

"You want me to meet you at the airport?"

"Not a chance."

Silence conveyed Kate's disappointment.

"I've got a better idea. Put on your prettiest dress and I'll have Foster drive straight from Kennedy to your apartment."

"We're going out?"

"Yes and no," Ben answered slowly. "There's a dinner I have to attend—a business association voted me their Man of the Year. To tell the truth, I'd forgotten all about it until Donald reminded me earlier. The ceremony'll be at the Rainbow Room tomorrow night."

The man had a schedule that could kill an ox. "Won't you be jet-lagged?"

"Probably. I'll get as much sleep as I can on the plane." Ben paused, then chuckled. "You could wear that blue dress you had on last week. I can guarantee that would keep me awake."

"Consider it done," Kate said blithely. There was no need to tell him that it was the only suitable dress she and Maggie had between them.

"Good. Then I'll see you tomorrow."

"Good night, Ben," Kate murmured. "Sweet dreams."

Ben sat in his suite at Claridge's looking at the receiver long after the connection had been broken. Sweet dreams indeed! With Kate as entrenched in his thoughts as she had been for the past month, he'd be lucky to get any sleep at all.

Right from the beginning, he recognized that he'd never met another woman like Kate. What he hadn't bargained on was how quickly her presence would insinuate itself into every aspect of his life. She was a constant source of contradiction—a mercurial woman who somehow stabilized his existence. He couldn't imagine what he'd ever do without her.

Was this love? Ben wondered. He wasn't sure. Up until now, there'd only been time in his life for brief affairs. Before Kate, he'd never known a woman who'd made him want to give more. But now it seemed he couldn't give enough—nor get enough.

He wanted Kate by his side—today, tomorrow, and every day after that. He wanted her committed to him forever. And if that wasn't love, it had to be damn close.

She'd never let him buy her a thing. Though he'd been piqued at the time, now he was rather pleased. Because that meant that the first gift she'd have from him would be the ice-white diamond solitaire he'd buy in Knightsbridge in the morning.

"I HOPE THIS DINNER won't be too awful." Sitting in the back seat of the Lincoln, Ben curled his arm around Kate's shoulders, holding her close to his side. He inhaled her hair's sweet, fresh smell. Since he'd picked her up ten minutes earlier, Ben hadn't been able to stop touching her. She didn't seem to mind a bit.

"It's you they're honoring," Kate said, tilting her face to his. "How can it help but be wonderful?"

"It can go on all night," Ben muttered. "And probably will." The ring—a brilliant-cut, three-karat solitaire—weighed heavily in his pocket. For now, it was his secret. Later, when they were finally alone, he'd bring it out and propose. "Do you think they'd notice if we cut out early?"

"Of course not. Two empty seats at the head table, no guest of honor in evidence—why should anybody notice that?"

"I suppose you're right." Ben sighed, resigning himself to a long evening as Foster pulled the car up to the entrance of Rockefeller Center. When the door was opened, he stepped out first, then turned to help Kate to her feet. Behind him came a flurry of comment as sightseers stopped to gawk at the limousine.

"Maude, look! A celebrity!"

"Who is it?"

"Damned if I know...."

Another voice chimed in. "It's that West man. Isn't he darling? Yoo-hoo, Ben! Over here!"

"He's shorter than he looks on TV...."

Ignoring one and all, Ben took Kate's arm and led her into the building. Without breaking stride, he headed for the bank of elevators that would take them to the top. She was shaking, and he tucked her under the sheltering curve of his arm as he hustled her into the empty car.

"It's all right now, Kate," Ben said softly. "They're gone."

"Thank God." To Ben's chagrin, she began to laugh. "I don't know how much longer I could have kept a straight face." Kate looked up at him, fluttering her eyelashes outrageously. "Yoo-hoo, Ben! Over here!"

"That woman was fifty if she was a day."

"But with wonderful taste." Her giggles erupted anew. "Does that happen often?"

"Often enough." Irritably Ben raked his fingers back through his hair. "I'm a public figure and it comes with the territory."

"Doesn't it bother you?"

"Sometimes." Ben shrugged. "Mostly I ignore it. I guess I've just gotten used to the fact that it happens."

"I'm not sure I like the idea of strange women calling you darling," Kate teased.

"I wouldn't worry if I were you," Ben said dryly. "She thought I was too short."

Kate poked him in the ribs for that, and he snaked his fingers beneath her coat and tickled her back. They were still laughing a moment later, when the elevator stopped and the doors slid open. Almost immediately they were swept forward into a sea of people, most of whom were eager to make Ben's acquaintance. Rescued from the crowd by the president of the association, they were escorted to their table and the testimonial began.

By eleven o'clock Kate knew the true meaning of the words boring and interminable. Dinner—warmed-over chicken Kiev accompanied by glutinous mashed potatoes—had been followed by speeches, Ben's among them. He'd been awarded a plaque, posed for pictures and shaken more hands than she cared to count. No doubt about it, the man was a model of patience.

Then he caught her eye from across the table and gave her a long, slow wink. Kate felt her stomach give a little lurch. It looked as if Ben's patience had just run out.

Kate had no idea how he managed things so efficiently, but in no time at all, he'd found their coats, said their goodbyes and hustled her off. The Lincoln was waiting at the curb, with Foster sitting behind the wheel, a cup of coffee in one hand and an adventure novel in the other. Seeing them, he quickly put them aside and snapped to attention.

The trip uptown was swift and silent. When they arrived at Westcon Plaza, Kate stepped out onto the sidewalk and inhaled deeply, drinking in the night air and enjoyed the relative solitude of the usually busy block.

Coming up beside her, Ben realized she was all he ever wanted. And more. "It's a beautiful night, isn't it?"

"Perfect."

Not yet, thought Ben. But it would be. She'd had so little romance in her life, so few of the frills that other women took for granted. All at once he knew that he wanted this night to be truly special, something Kate would never forget.

"Let's not go in just yet." Taking her arm, he began to walk.

"Where are we going?"

"You'll see."

Across from them lay Central Park. At its southernmost boundary, opposite the Plaza Hotel, was where the horsedrawn carriages waited for hire. By this time of night, most had gone home. The one that remained, a shiny landau drawn by a sedate-looking gray horse, was preparing to leave. A hundred-dollar bill, passed to the driver, changed his mind.

Ben helped Kate up into the seat, then climbed in beside her. There was a lap rug lying on the seat opposite and he took it and spread it over them both.

Kate's eyes shone as the driver clucked and shook his whip and the horse moved into his steady, leisurely trot. "How did you know I always wanted to ride in one of these?"

Ben's arm curled around her and pressed her close. "Lucky guess?"

"My foot," Kate replied affably. "Sometimes I think you're too smart for you own good."

"Oh?" Ben's brow lifted. "And what do you think the rest of the time?"

"That I love you anyway."

They both were silent for a moment. Then Ben's hand lifted to Kate's chin and tilted her face to his. "Do you mean that, Kate?"

He saw the answer in her eyes and his heart began to pound.

"Yes," she said.

"Sweetest Kate..." The first touch of Ben's lips upon hers was light, almost tentative. But Kate opened her mouth and drew him to her. Their passion quickly escalated; moments later, when he pulled back, she was breathless and aching with frustration.

"Don't stop . . ." she murmured.

Ben looked meaningfully at the driver's back. Beneath the blanket, he slid a hand onto her thigh. "Maybe this wasn't such a good idea, after all."

"Maybe not." Kate gasped as Ben's hand began to move, stroking, kneading, sending flashes of heat searing through her. "What will he think if we ask him to take us back?"

"That we can't wait another minute." Ben grinned and signaled the driver to turn around. Then he kissed Kate again, long and hard. When they parted, they were still two blocks from home. "I wonder if that damn horse can move any faster."

In spite of herself, Kate smiled. "I thought this mode of transportation might be a little primitive for you."

"Oh, I don't know." As the carriage turned the last corner, Ben was already preparing to descend. "Now that we're here, I have a feeling you're about to find out just how very primitive I can be."

THE SUN AWAKENED Kate the next morning. Bright streamers of light shone in through the French doors on one side of the bedroom, warming the bed. Beside her, Ben was still asleep, his face turned into the pillow, the plaid comforter snuggled up to his chin.

Kate started to reach for him, then paused, smiling. After last night, no doubt Ben needed all the rest he could get.

Save for a single light burning in the foyer, the apartment had been dark when they stumbled in, wrapped in each other's arms and frantic as teenagers in the back seat of a Chevy. A long kiss in the elevator had had them so engrossed that on the first try, they'd missed their stop entirely. It wasn't until the car had returned them to the lobby that Ben had looked up and seen what had happened.

This time when the elevator had delivered them to the penthouse, he'd swept her through the door and guided her straight to the bedroom. They'd flung off their clothes and tumbled to the bed together.

The time apart had only strengthened their desire, and Kate had found herself overwhelmed by the intensity of Ben's lovemaking. By turns, he'd been both rough and gentle, bringing them to the edge and back, again and again, before letting go.

Afterward, as the sound of their ragged breathing filled the darkened room, Ben had shifted to lie beside her. His drooping eyelids had told Kate he was struggling to stay awake.

"What time is it in London?" she'd asked, her fingers tracing a feather-light line down the side of his jaw.

"Five in the morning." Ben was remembering the ring still waiting in his pocket, and had smiled dreamily. "You should be asleep."

"Not yet. I have something for you."

He'd tried to get up, but Kate had forestalled the effort. Gently she'd pushed him back down, then pulled the quilt over him. "Whatever it is," she'd said, "it can wait till morning."

"But—"

"No buts." She'd placed her fingertip over his lips, holding them closed until she saw she had his acquiescence. Smiling then, Kate had snuggled down beside him. "I love you, Ben," she whispered.

His arm had curled around her possessively and he'd pulled her close. "I love you, too," he'd murmured, his voice heavy with sleep. He'd hugged her to him, hard, and moments later they were both asleep.

Now, hours later in the sun-brightened room, Kate wondered whether Ben would remember his declaration when he awoke. "You'd better," she muttered, climbing out of bed. She found his robe on the back of the closet door and pulled it on, rolling back the sleeves and cinching the belt tight, before heading for the bedroom door. She'd brew a pot of coffee and bring in a cup for Ben to wake up to. The prospect of performing such a simple domestic chore pleased her enormously.

The night before, she had seen nothing of Ben's apartment and now, as she padded barefoot through the rooms, she took it all in—the living room was all antiques and silk brocade; the library—a smaller, more informal room—was done in cherry-wood and chintz.

After three wrong turns, Kate finally found herself in the dining room. From there it was an easy matter to push through the swinging door into the kitchen. The aroma of fresh coffee filled the air, the Sunday *Times* was waiting on the counter, and a single place-setting had been laid at the small oak table by the window.

Kate jumped as a door on the other side of the room swung inward and Parker emerged from the pantry carrying a five-pound bag of sugar. "You nearly gave me heart failure, Parker!"

The houseman looked equally startled. "And you, me." He laid the bag down on the counter. "I didn't know anyone was here but Mr. West."

"Yes . . . Well . . ." Feeling ridiculously underdressed, Kate clutched at the lapels of the gaping robe. "I thought you lived in Wilton."

"When Mr. West is there, I do. When he's in Manhattan, so am I."

Imagine having someone whose only duty was to follow you around and see to your comfort, thought Kate. She could hardly fathom such a thing, while Ben obviously took this kind of luxury for granted. She loved him. And he'd said he loved her. But would two people who were poles apart ever be able to meet in the middle?

"Shall I lay another place?" Parker asked.

"No . . ." Kate looked around and located the coffee-maker on the counter. "Actually, I just came in for some coffee. Two cups and a tray, if you would."

In no time at all, Kate was on her way back to Ben's room. She'd left the door ajar and now she saw that Ben was awake, sitting up in bed and leaning against a pillow he'd propped against the headboard.

As she entered the room, he looked up and greeted her with a smile. "I was wondering where you'd got to."

"I found the kitchen." Kate answered his smile with one of her own. "It's three blocks down and two over." She set the tray over Ben's legs, then climbed onto the bed beside him.

"Are you complaining about the size of my apartment?"

"Who, me?" Kate asked innocently. She blew on her coffee, then took a cautious sip. Ben was uncharacteristically still, leaving his cup untouched on the tray. He watched her, his expression curiously intent. Slightly unnerved, Kate put down her cup.

"Is something wrong?"

"No," Ben replied slowly. "Actually, I think something is very right. And if you don't like my apartment, you may feel free to make any changes you wish, short of moving us bag and baggage into that glorified closet you call home."

"Ben," Kate queried softly, "what are you talking about?"

He reached across the sheet and took her hand in his. "I want you to be happy, Kate. And I want you to be comfortable. . . . And I want you to be my wife."

Stunned, she stared at him, feeling as though the wind had been knocked out of her. Then she was overcome by a rush of happiness.

"I . . . You . . . *what?*"

"Marry me, Kate," Ben said. He reached beneath the pillow and drew out a small black velvet box. He flipped it open and a large white diamond sparkled there.

"Oh, my Lord!" Kate breathed. "I guess you weren't talking in your sleep."

"When?"

"Last night." Kate stared at the diamond. "You told me that you loved me. But you were really almost asleep, and I wasn't sure if you meant it."

"Be sure," Ben told her. "Because I've never been so sure of anything in my life. I love you, Kate. And I want you with me, always." He smiled as he slipped the diamond from its nest and held it out to her. "You can touch it, you know. It won't bite."

She accepted the ring. "That's got to be the biggest diamond I've ever seen."

Ben shrugged. "Someday I'll introduce you to Elizabeth Taylor."

Maybe it was the very casualness of his comment, or the value of the diamond she held in her hand, but all at once Kate was stricken by doubts. This morning she'd awakened in a fantasy world—a penthouse beyond her wildest imagining, servants, and now a diamond the size of a marble. Everything seemed to be moving much too fast.

"I couldn't possibly wear something so big." Kate handed him back the ring. "I'd feel silly."

"You'll be my wife," Ben said gently. "It'll be just right." He took her left hand and slipped the diamond on to her third finger. "Do you love me, Kate?"

She looked up into his eyes. The warmth and caring she saw mirrored there touched her. "You know I do."

"Then nothing else matters." He took both hands and held them. "You haven't given me an answer, you know. Will you marry me, Kate?"

Ben wasn't aware he'd been holding his breath until she began to smile and he knew what her answer would be. Love coursed through him as Kate rose up on her knees and touched her lips to his.

"Yes, Ben," she answered softly. "I will."

12

KATE HAD INITIATED the embrace, but now she was the one who found herself folded into Ben's arms. The sheet slipped down to his waist as he pulled her against the solid wall of his chest. Leisurely they shared a kiss.

"How about June?" Ben murmured, his lips pressed to the hollow of her throat.

Kate laughed huskily, shifting her weight so that her body covered his. "How about now?"

"Impatient, are you?" Ben's hands slipped inside the robe to cup her breasts. "I like that in a woman."

"You'd better." Kate gasped as his thumb and forefinger closed over her nipple, kneading it gently. "June—" she exhaled slowly "—would be fine. Anytime..."

Ben smiled, enjoying her response. That he wanted her again didn't surprise him; that the wanting seemed beyond his control, did. He lifted her breasts in his palms, supporting their firm weight as his thumbs brushed slowly back and forth over their rosy tips. Then Kate arched against him, driving their hips together.

"The sooner the better," Ben growled. "I'll have my lawyer draw up the papers in the morning."

It took a moment for the words to sink in. Even then, Kate wasn't sure what she'd heard. "What papers?"

Ben frowned at the clumsy way he had brought up the subject. And his timing wasn't exactly the best, either. Kate was staring at him, and judging from the look on her face, neither of them was going anywhere until she had some answers.

"Just a standard agreement," Ben said finally. "Nothing out of the ordinary."

"A prenuptial agreement?" Kate rolled away from him.

"Well . . . Yes."

"And that's *nothing* out of the ordinary?"

Perversely, the angrier her expression grew, the more determined Ben became to deal with the issue and resolve it now. "Think of it as a form of protection—a piece of paper that will look out for both our interests in the future."

"Both our interests?" Kate sat up and wrapped her robe tightly around her.

"Of course. The document spells out what each of us has brought into the marriage and what each will take out. You'll be very well provided for, Kate."

In frustration, she punched him in the arm. "What you mean is that I'll be very well provided for in case of divorce."

"Exactly."

"So, what you really mean is that you don't expect this marriage to last."

"That's not what I said—"

"Dammit, Ben. You didn't have to say it." Kate struggled with the ring and wrenched it off. "The very fact that you feel we need a prenuptial agreement says it all."

"You're deliberately misunderstanding this. A prenup is a form of insurance, nothing more. I don't expect my buildings to burn down, but that doesn't mean I don't buy coverage."

"I don't want insurance," Kate retorted, pounding the ring into the pillow between them. "I want love, and a marriage that will last forever. And a man who believes in that love."

"I do love you, Kate," Ben said slowly. "And I do believe in us. But what I don't believe in is mixing business with personal relationships. I've tried it before and it just doesn't work. I would do anything I could to make you happy. By the same token, I want—no, I need for you to do this one thing for me."

Kate knew he was remembering his dealings with his father. Still, that didn't make it hurt any less. She didn't give a damn about the contract and being "provided for" by Ben's money. What she did need was Ben's trust. Without that, what kind of a future could they possibly have together?

"I don't want your money, Ben. I never have."

"I know that."

Kate got out of bed. Her clothes were scattered on the floor and she gathered them into her arms. "Then don't ask me to sign away my dreams."

"Are you telling me you refuse?"

"Yes . . . I guess I am."

"Dammit, Kate!" Ben swore with frustration. "You're trying to manipulate me."

"No, I'm not," Kate insisted, starting for the bathroom. "I'm trying to love you. But at the moment, you're not making it easy."

"You're being impossible!"

"I guess that makes two of us," she responded grimly.

The door closed behind her. Ben clenched his fist and slammed it into the pillow. The diamond ring bounced up, then tumbled to the floor, forgotten.

MAGGIE HAD BEEN squawking about one thing or another ever since Kate had gotten home ten minutes earlier. Now Kate had silenced her—at least momentarily—with a fierce glare.

Nasty looks, however, hadn't been enough when Kate had stripped off the sheath she had borrowed from Maggie and tossed it into a corner. "You know," Maggie commented, "that's my dress you've just thrown away like a used tissue."

"Sorry," Kate snapped, pulling on an old sweat suit in its stead.

"I can tell." Maggie retrieved the dress and shook it out. "Tough night, huh?"

It would only be a matter of time before Maggie wormed the whole thing out of her. Kate figured that she might as well get it over with. "Ben asked me to marry him."

"Glory hallelujah!" Maggie tossed the dress up in the air. "I'm going to be a bridesmaid at the wedding of the decade."

"There isn't going to be any wedding."

"You're going to elope? How romantic! Imagine being swept off your feet by Benjamin West. Where's he taking you? The Riviera? Bora Bora?"

"Ben isn't taking me anywhere. We're not getting married."

"You're not getting married." Maggie stuck a fingertip in her ear and jiggled it for effect. "Run that by me again, would you? I think I missed something."

"Your hearing is just fine. Ben asked me to marry him, and I turned him down."

"Now I get it," Maggie said. "I'm fine, and *you're* the one who's crazy."

"Not crazy," Kate corrected. She walked over to the kitchen counter for a cup of coffee. "Mad."

"Pardon me if I don't see the distinction."

"Mad as in angry, not nuts. Ben says he wants to marry me, but first I have to sign a prenuptial agreement."

"So?"

"So I'm not going to."

"That's my girl. Reasonable as ever."

Kate spun around. "It's so much not the document itself, but the fact that he seems to think we need it. How can I marry a man who's already planning his own divorce?"

"Ben's a businessman," Maggie said reasonably. "It's probably second nature to him to want to plan for all eventualities. That doesn't mean he expects them to happen."

It was more or less the same thing Ben had said himself. Kate remained unconvinced. Spying her sneakers under the table, she sat down and began to lace them on. "Businessmen," she pointed out, "look at the bottom line. And the bottom line here is that he doesn't trust me. If he did, none of this would be necessary."

"Does he love you?"

Kate looked up, surprised at how easily the question made her smile. "He says he does."

"That's a hell of a start," Maggie commented. "Lots of woman would have settled for less."

"I'm not lots of women."

"Thank goodness for that." Maggie watched as Kate stood and headed for the door. "Now where are you going?"

"For a run. It's the best thing for relieving tension."

Maggie stared in surprise. "Planning on racing up and down the stairs?"

"Of course not. I'm going to the park. Ten times around the reservoir."

"That's ten miles!"

Kate pulled open the door. "That should just about do."

"Kate Hallaby, you've never jogged a step in your life!"

"Then it's high time I started."

Maggie sighed loudly and looked around for her sneakers. "I guess if you're going to go out and kill yourself, the least I can do is come along and pick up the pieces. But I'm warning you," she added, shaking a finger in Kate's direction, "I've changed my mind about being a bridesmaid."

"Good."

"Maid of honor," Maggie grumbled, tying on her shoes. "*And* I get to pick my own dress."

"What's the matter? Don't you like my taste?"

"In men, yes." Maggie smiled sweetly. "And of course, we all know how well you're doing with the one you've got...."

Kate slammed the door firmly behind them.

"Lead the way," Maggie said resignedly. "We may as well get this over with."

KATE RETURNED from her run as unsettled as she'd been at the outset. Her anger had dissipated, but the tension remained. And the apprehension. If she'd done the right thing, why did it feel so terribly wrong?

More than anything, Kate wanted to accept Ben's proposal. The thought of becoming his wife, of being by his side every day for the rest of their lives, filled her with joy. But she couldn't get past her belief that a marriage requiring a contract was one that was bound to founder.

That there was a good reason for Ben's wariness only made things more difficult. But not impossible! She'd never backed down from a challenge before, and she wasn't about to start now. Whether he knew it or not, Benjamin West was about to meet his match.

AT SEVEN ON MONDAY morning, Kate was at the garage. Ben hadn't told her she didn't have a job, so she intended to assume that she did. She passed Foster on the way in and he shrugged and told her his shift had been quiet. With that in mind, Kate went into the lounge, opened a book, and prepared for a wait.

It didn't last long.

"There's a pickup for you in front of Westcon Plaza ASAP," Julio called from the office half an hour later. "Three men, including Mr. West. Destination's a construction site downtown."

"Got it." Kate twisted her hair up under her cap and went to get the car. Five minutes later, she circled the block and pulled up smoothly before the gilded double doors.

Ben knew she was coming and yet wasn't prepared. As Kate stepped out of the Lincoln, he found himself gazing at her with a hunger he was powerless to control. He never should have let her walk away from him the day before, he reflected. Not that she'd given him much choice. No, being Kate, she'd simply up and left.

For now, she was there. But without his ring on her finger, without his name joined to her own, how long could that be expected to last? She wasn't cut out for the life she was living. At most, a few more months and she'd be gone. Already it was May. Come September, a new semester would start and she'd leave him forever.

He'd offered her his love. And he'd offered her his hand in marriage. There had to be a way to make her see reason about the contract. He refused to believe there wasn't.

Ben hung back as his two associates slipped into the back seat. "We have to talk," he said to Kate. "When this is done, park the car and come to my office."

"Yes, sir!" Kate snapped, irked by his preemptory tone. No doubt he had his papers all ready for her to sign. Good luck, she thought, slipping in behind the wheel. He was going to need it.

Kate used every shortcut she knew, but the trip downtown took twenty minutes. She could hear the conversation in the back seat, picking up enough to realize that the two men accompanying Ben were Mort Silverburg and Ozzie Green, partners in the nightclub project that he'd been concerned about for some time. From Ben's tone, it was evident that he was no more pleased with their company now than he had been in the past.

Finally she reached their destination, a building lot on a busy corner. Wire fencing, emblazoned with the familiar red-and-white Westcon signs, had gone up along the sidewalk. Inside, a large cement mixer was pouring a foundation. Engrossed in their discussion, the three men got out and walked quickly onto the site.

There was an empty space beside a fire hydrant, and Kate pulled the Lincoln there and waited. She watched as Green and Silverburg conferred with the job foreman while Ben, carrying a roll of plans under his arm, disappeared inside the trailer that served as an office. More than an hour passed before he emerged.

Ben had met up with Green and Silverburg and they were heading for the gate, when a woman opened the door to the trailer and called Ben back. This time he was only inside for a moment before joining the other two men on the curb. "I won't be going back uptown with you," he told them. "It seems I've got a meeting on 29th. Kate, if you could drop me there? And then take these gentlemen anywhere they wish."

"Of course." Kate opened the door, waited until all three men were settled inside, then shut it softly. Obviously her meeting with Ben would have to be postponed. It was probably just as well, since she hadn't changed her mind about a thing. They were bound to argue again and she, for one, was in no hurry about it.

She dropped Ben on the corner he indicated, then awaited further instructions. Finally Green leaned forward over the back of the seat. "Three-fifty Central Park West," he said, and Kate put the car in Drive.

Kate wound her way through the heavy morning traffic, keeping one eye on the road and the other on the rearview mirror. Though the two men spoke in hushed tones, it was obvious that a heated argument was taking place in the back seat. As she cruised slowly up Columbus Avenue, their voices rose in volume until she was able to catch snatches of the conversation.

"You're being paranoid!" Silverburg barked, and though Kate missed Green's reply, she did hear him say a moment later, "You try telling that to the plan examiner. Sure, it was a lot of money. But we got what we wanted—"

He broke off as he glanced in Kate's direction, his eye catching hers in the mirror.

Silverburg looked out the window. "Right here. This'll do."

Kate guided the Lincoln over to the curb. Before she could open the door, the two men had gathered up their things and scrambled out. Green paused, his eyes narrowing as they searched her face.

He was obviously curious about how much she'd heard, and how much she'd understood. Any doubts Kate might have had about the importance of the conversation vanished. Meeting his gaze, she gathered the bubble gum she was chewing into a large wad at the front of her mouth and blew gently. The bubble expanded almost to her nose before popping with a loud crack. To her satisfaction, Green turned away in disgust.

Kate waited until they had disappeared into the throng of people jamming the sidewalk, before climbing back behind the wheel. No further instructions had been called in, so she returned the car to the garage. An hour later, the call she'd been waiting for came.

It took her five minutes to walk to Westcon Plaza, and another two in the elevator. She'd expected to find Jody waiting for her. Instead, Ben himself was there.

"Come on," he said, grasping her arm and hurrying her along the corridor.

Kate had to trot to keep up. "What's the hurry?"

"This." Ben slammed the door to his office behind them, then pushed her up against it. Kate melted into his arms as his lips crushed down on hers for a kiss that left them both weak. Her cap tipped off and her hair tumbled free. Ben's fingers burrowed in its heavy strands as he held her to him.

"Dammit," he muttered. "You make me crazy."

Pressed tightly between Ben and the door, Kate felt herself relax, the tension that had been with her for the last twenty-four hours draining away. There was desperation in the way he'd trapped her there, and determination, too, which thrilled Kate. As long as Ben cared, as long as he loved her, somehow they'd work things out.

"Crazy?" Kate thrust her hips forward and moved against him. "Is that what you call it?"

Ben chuckled softly, even as his hands grasped her hips and gently pushed her away. "I invited you up here to talk."

"Oh, we'll talk, all right." Kate smiled. Her hands dropped to his belt buckle. "Later."

"Kate!" She had slipped her fingers inside his fly. Then Ben pulled her to him. He kissed her lips, her throat, the slope of her breasts. Even through the clothing that separated them, he could feel her body's simmering response.

As Ben reached around behind her and flipped the latch on the door, Kate undid his pants and slid them off. He was hard and ready. Leaning down, Kate pressed a kiss to the swirl of dark hair below his navel. Then her tongue curled over the elastic band of his briefs.

He could feel her breath, hot and moist, upon him. He'd meant for them to talk, but by God, he could barely even think. The muscles of his stomach clenched as she drew her tongue over the thin layer of cotton between them. Heat poured through him, bringing with it a desire so intense that it bordered on pain.

Ben grasped Kate's shoulders and hauled her to her feet. They worked together, their fingers stumbling over each other, as they made short work of first her clothing, then his. This was no time for finesse and gentle caresses. It was urgent need, pure and simple.

Ben lifted Kate high, then slowly lowered her over him. Kate locked her legs around his hips and fought for each gasping breath.

She'd never felt so alive, nor so gloriously complete. Then Ben began to move. She arched her back in response, and her muscles tensed, becoming almost rigid. Desire consumed her, blotting out everything.

Ben felt Kate shudder beneath his hands, and he smothered her cry with his lips as her spasms touched off his own climax. He lost himself in release.

Moments passed before Ben realized that they were still just inside the door to his office. Kate's back was pressed against the wall, her legs wrapped around his hips, and her face was nestled against his shoulder. He stroked her hair.

"I'll bet you think I'm going to sign those papers now," she murmured.

Laughing, Ben gathered her close. "Sweet Kate, if there's one thing I've learned, it's that whatever I want you to do, you'll undoubtedly do the opposite."

"You mean you've changed your mind?"

"No, but I have decided to give you as much time as it takes to change yours. We're good together, Kate. You can't deny it. We make a hell of a team, and we're going to have one hell of a marriage, just as soon as you stop letting that piece of paper stand in our way."

Kate unwound herself from Ben's embrace. Piece by piece, she gathered her clothing up. "Has it occurred to you that maybe you're the one who's put a stumbling block in our way?"

"Not a stumbling block," Ben corrected firmly. "A precaution. One that any sane person in my position would take."

She might as well argue with a rock. Ben believed in his position just as strongly as she believed in hers. There had to be a way to make him change his mind, but for the life of her, she hadn't the slightest idea what it was.

Instead, as she rose and pulled on her clothes, Kate deliberately changed the subject. The conversation she'd overheard was important, and she was sure that Ben would want to know about it. She proceeded while he listened in silence until she'd finished, his scowl growing more and more pronounced with each passing moment.

"You're sure of everything you've told me?" he asked when she was done.

Kate stepped into her shoes and picked up her cap. "As sure as an eavesdropper can be. They kept their voices low, so I only caught bits and pieces. Still, it seemed to me that they were arguing about a payoff— one they had no desire for you to know about."

Ben swore. "I knew something had to be going on. It just didn't make sense the way the permit eased through so suddenly after being held up in the Building Department for months."

Kate coiled her hair and tucked it under her cap. "What will you do?"

Ben was already striding toward his desk. "I needed a trail to follow, and I've got that now. Those two aren't the only ones with government connections."

"Ben?"

He stopped and turned.

"If your partners paid somebody off, you're in it up to your neck."

"I know." Ben grinned. It was the last thing Kate expected. "This one's going to be a challenge."

"Want some help?"

Slowly he shook his head. "This is my problem, not yours. If we were married—" he let the thought dangle meaningfully for a moment "—things might be different."

"That's coercion."

Ben shrugged. "I'm not above it."

She smiled sweetly. "I never thought you were."

Behind his desk, Ben was already reaching for his phone. "I suspect I'm going to be busy for the next few days. Take the time and think about us. I believe in you, Kate. All we need now is for you to believe in me."

Kate unlatched the door and drew it open. "Are you sure you'll be all right?"

"I'll be all right." Ben trapped the receiver between his shoulder and ear and punched out a number. "Trust me, Kate."

"I do," she said softly, and closed the door between them.

13

TRUE TO HIS WORD, Ben was busy. Over the next four days, Kate drove him uptown, downtown, and everywhere in between. Though she was anxious about his predicament, Ben didn't seem worried. Instead he rose to this newest challenge like a man who thrived on adversity.

Watching him in action made Kate's pulse race. And watching was all she was allowed to do, because Ben was determined to give her time to think. Though they saw each other daily, he was careful to observe the propriety of their respective positions. There were no more picnic breakfasts or moonlit dinners, no suggestive winks or furtive caresses.

In short, thought Kate, he'd taken away all her fun.

There was a method to his madness. Obviously Ben was waiting for her to come to her senses and sign that ridiculous piece of paper. However, Kate had no intention of signing and every intention of talking him around to her way of thinking. She'd do it, too—just as soon as the more urgent matter of clearing up his business affairs was completed. They were planning for the rest of their lives, after all. What difference could a few days possibly make?

Friday morning, Donald called her at the garage. "Do you know who Crash Armstrong is?" he asked.

"Of course," Kate replied, picturing the young, sexy rock star whose last three albums had gone platinum.

"He's headlining the show this week at the casino. He was supposed to fly direct to Atlantic City, but he missed his connection and he's coming into Kennedy instead. I need you to pick him up at noon and drive him down to the Jersey shore."

"No problem."

"Yeah, I'll bet." Donald chuckled. "It'll probably be pretty late by the time you're done, so if you want to stay over and come back tomorrow, go ahead. I'll have the resort hold a room in your name."

"Thanks," said Kate. At the moment she was only killing time in New York. A change of scenery might be just what she needed. "I think I'll take you up on that."

At noon, Kate arrived at the airport. As usual, Kennedy was packed with travelers. She left the car waiting at the curb and hurried inside, spotting Crash as he emerged from the VIP elevator. He was tall and lean, with long, shiny dark hair and the chiseled features of a hawk. Already people were beginning to stop and gape, and Kate hurried to his side, hoping to get him outside before they were mobbed.

"Hi," she greeted, reaching for his suitcase. "I'm your driver. The car's just outside."

"*You're* taking me to Atlantic City?" A slow, sensual smile lit his face. "Well, love, aren't we lucky?"

"Maybe." Kate grinned right back at him. "And maybe not." She saw a trio of teenagers heading their way. "I think that depends on how quickly we manage to get ourselves out of here."

"In that case," Crash drawled, taking her arm, "I'm all yours."

When they reached the car, Kate stowed his gear in the trunk while Crash helped himself to the front seat. "You might be more comfortable in the back," she suggested, slipping in beside him. "There's a TV, the refrigerator's stocked, and there's plenty of room to spread out if you want to take a nap."

"Don't worry about me— I'm used to going without sleep. I'd rather enjoy the company." He settled back against the plush seat as Kate pulled the car out into traffic. "Will you be in Atlantic City for the weekend?"

Kate shook her head. "Only tonight. I'll be heading back in the morning."

"You will come and see my show."

His self-confidence made her smile. "Maybe. Is it any good?"

"Good? It's terrific."

"Maybe I'll fit it in, then."

"Do that." Crash's arm, resting across the back of the seat, lifted casually. "I'll see that you get a pass." A finger slipped beneath the back of her cap, tipping it off so that Kate's hair tumbled free.

Kate kept both eyes on the road. "Take your hand off my neck," she said.

"Why?"

"Because I don't want it there."

"You have lovely hair."

She shot him a look. "The man I'm seeing thinks so."

"Oh." The hand fell away.

They rode for several minutes in silence. At that rate, Kate reflected, it was going to be a very long drive. "Do you always do that?" she asked.

"Do what?"

"Make a play for every woman you meet."

"Not every woman." Crash smiled innocently. "Just the hot ones."

Kate laughed. "It's part of your public image, right?"

"Sure." The smile widened into a grin. "The part I like best."

She could see how he'd sold so many millions of records, thought Kate. The man was impossibly appealing—a fact his self-confidence only underscored. "I guess you don't have many woman friends."

"I guess not," Crash agreed. "Who has the time?"

"You do." Kate smiled sweetly. "We've got four hours before we reach Atlantic City."

"You really don't want me to seduce you, then?"

His tone hit just the right note of wistful disappointment. No doubt he'd been charming women out of their pants for years. Kate shook her head.

"This man of yours—is it serious?"

"Very."

"Are you in love with him?"

Kate cast an eye in his direction. "Is that any of your business?"

"Sure." Crash grinned. "I'm trying to gauge my chances."

"Take my word for it. You have no chance."

"Well, then," said Crash, leaning back, "you are. Does he love you?"

"I think so."

"True love. How sweet. I've written songs about it."

"You've also written songs about lying and cheating."

Crash looked pleased. "So you do like my music."

"Some of it." Kate put on her blinker and turned onto the expressway. "I like the love songs better."

"You're a romantic."

"I like a happy ending."

"The sad ones sell better," he told her. "They're more true to life. Look at the statistics—nobody's willing to work at a relationship anymore. They want everything handed to them. It's quite sad, really."

Though the conversation soon shifted to other topics, Crash's words stayed with Kate throughout the rest of the long drive. When they reached the resort, Crash went off to do a sound check, and Kate signed in. Then she changed her clothes and strolled out to the boardwalk. Bound on one side by the ocean and on the other by a row of small shops and hotels, the wide-plank walkway was a feast of sights and sounds.

At another time, Kate would have found it fascinating. Today, however, she was too distracted to appreciate it. She stopped at a small seaside café for dinner, then went back to the hotel for Crash's show. As she listened to him play his first set, she mulled over what he'd said earlier.

Was his characterization of her and Ben true? Were they both so intent on having things their own way that they'd allowed their relationship to suffer as a result? Certainly they'd both been adamant in their demands—demands that they each expected the other to ultimately bend to.

But what she wanted wasn't unreasonable. What was love without trust? And how could a marriage be expected to survive without a combination of the two? It was a partnership in every sense of the word....

Kate recalled the last time she and Ben had been alone together: in his office at the beginning of the week, when she'd told him what his business associates were up to. Though he'd questioned her carefully, he'd never doubted her. Indeed, Ben had never—at any point— made her feel that she didn't have his trust. He'd opened up his life to her, sharing business and personal confidences alike. He believed in her, he'd told her when they parted that night. It was she who had to learn to believe in him.

Now, to her consternation, Kate admitted that it wasn't Ben she doubted, but herself. She'd been scared by the depth of her own feelings, and was unable to believe that Ben could actually feel the same. After all, who was she? No Cinderella, certainly; just plain old Kate Hallaby from Brooklyn.

She'd been afraid. And mention of a prenuptial agreement had only aggravated those fears. She'd accused Ben of planning ahead for his own divorce; but what was she doing if not the same? If she'd truly believed that she could make their marriage work, what did it matter if she signed the paper or not?

Kate sat up straighter in her chair. She'd always prided herself on her guts and her tenacity, so where were they now when she needed them most? All she'd done so far was take the coward's way out. Worse, by doing so, she'd allowed herself to jeopardize the only thing that really mattered—her relationship with Ben.

Let Ben draw up his document. She'd sign the damn thing and he could lock it away in his vault. With a little hard work, some luck and plenty of compromise, they could take it out and burn it on their fiftieth wedding anniversary.

Crash was doing his last number when Kate slipped out. She hurried upstairs and tossed the few things she'd brought back into her suitcase. Driving full speed, it would still be one in the morning by the time she got back to New York. Ben would be in bed, and the picture made her smile.

Maybe she'd wake him up, and then again maybe she wouldn't. Perhaps she'd just snuggle in beside him and let things go from there. Either way, it was going to be a memorable night.

BEN HUNG UP THE PHONE and sat back in his desk chair, smiling with satisfaction. It was done. He'd finally managed to straighten things out—or at least come close enough that he wouldn't awaken anytime soon to marshalls at his door and lurid headlines in the *National Investigator.*

His ex-partners had indeed made the payoffs he'd accused them of, and considering the quality of the work they'd been planning to do, no wonder. As a result of Ben's probing into their affairs, two previous projects were now under investigation, as well. As of yesterday, Ben's partnership with Green and Silverburg was irrevocably dissolved. He'd bought out their interest in the land and put the proposal for the nightclub on hold indefinitely.

He'd finished fulfilling the responsibilities that couldn't wait. Now he was on his own time, and that meant only one thing: Kate.

He'd thought a week would be long enough to bring her to her senses. Little had he dreamed that it would bring him to his, instead. But if the past five days had shown him anything, it was that he needed her in his life. On his terms. On her terms. On any terms at all.

Always, before, he'd had his work to sustain him. He'd thrived on the excitement and the travel and the challenge. He'd lived to make the next deal, feeling heady with conquest the same way some men felt about sex.

A week ago, he'd believed that with a problem like the nightclub partnership to occupy his energies and his time, he wouldn't miss Kate at all. He couldn't have been more wrong.

How could he have known that it wasn't his work that would give him sustenance, but rather those all-too-brief moments he saw her each day? No matter how busy he'd been, she'd never been out of his thoughts. No matter how absorbed he became, a piece of him always remained with her.

To hell with the agreement. Kate was part of him, his other half. He could no more protect his business from her than he could himself. If he didn't have Kate, he might as well have nothing. With her, he would have it all.

The ring was upstairs in his apartment. According to Donald, Kate was in Atlantic City. He could be there in three hours, maybe less if he pushed it. He'd track Kate down and then, by God, he'd put that ring back on her finger where it belonged. No more arguing, no more discussion. Kate had had things her own way long enough. Now it was going to be his turn.

Half an hour later, Ben was on the Garden State Parkway heading south. To his chagrin, however, when he called ahead to the resort, it was only to be told that although Kate Hallaby had checked in earlier, she had since checked out. "Where did she go?" Ben demanded.

"I heard her say something about home," the desk clerk stammered. "Then she had the car brought up and left."

Ben's next call was to Donald. "I hope I'm not interrupting anything," he said, aware of the late hour.

"You are," Donald replied. "So what else is new?"

Ben grinned. "Monday morning, you can give yourself a raise. In the meantime, I've got something I want you to do."

KATE WAS NEARING Long Branch when the call came. She'd been driving for almost two hours on the dark, near-empty turnpike. The miles passed in a blur as she concentrated on only one thing—getting back to New York in the shortest possible time. The last thing she expected at that hour was for her phone to ring.

Kate lifted the receiver.

"Kate? It's Donald. I have an errand for you."

"No, you don't," she said firmly. "It's almost midnight. I'm off duty, remember?"

"Come on, you're already in the car."

"I'm an hour's drive from the city, Donald. Whatever you want, it'll have to wait."

"No, it won't, What I need is for you to pick up a passenger on the Garden State. There's a rest-stop up ahead of you. Your passenger is already there."

"Did someone's car break down?"

"Something like that," Donald muttered evasively. "Just pull in and park. He'll be waiting for you."

"Who?" asked Kate, but the line was already dead.

She reset the receiver. If she'd had any idea at all where Donald was, she'd be more than a little tempted to call him back and give him a piece of her mind. The last thing she needed was this sort of delay!

Ten minutes later, Kate saw the sign announcing an upcoming rest stop. Reluctantly she turned on her blinker. She drove past the restaurant and the gas pumps, then pulled into a parking space in a well-lighted corner of the lot. She'd barely turned off the ignition when the passenger door was opened from the outside.

"Hi, Kate," Ben said quietly.

His hair was ruffled, his collar turned up against the night. There were dark circles under his eyes and a show of stubble along his jaw. Kate's heart swelled at the sight of him. She'd been running to Ben and doing so gladly. But the fact that he was willing to meet her halfway meant a lot.

Surprise, hope, love—the combination left her speechless. Kate's smile, however, said it all.

Ben slipped onto the front seat and closed the door behind him. The dome light went off, leaving them in semidarkness. "Is this car available for out-of-town trips?" he drawled.

Grinning, Kate leaned close to brush her lips over his. "Mister, I'll take you anywhere you want to go."

Ben opened his arms and Kate slid into them. He held her cradled close against his chest. She might not know it yet, but he had no intention of ever letting go. "I'm hardly likely to turn down an offer like that."

"I hope not," Kate teased, tilting her face up to his. "I've been thinking—"

"Don't even say it," Ben interrupted. "The more you think, the more we argue. I'm finished arguing with you, Kate. And I'm done chasing you all over town. We're getting married, and that's that."

Kate didn't mean to smile, but she couldn't seem to help it. "Is that an order?"

"Yes! No . . . Actually, it's a request."

"I could tell."

"You're making fun of me again."

"No," Kate said. "I'm just enjoying . . . us." She watched as Ben reached into his pocket and pulled out her ring. For the second time, the beauty of the diamond took her breath away.

Ben lifted Kate's hand and slipped the ring on her finger. "That's where it belongs, and that's where it will stay. You're mine, Kate. Forever."

"And you are mine," Kate told him, looking down at their joined hands.

"It's about time you admitted that." Ben rather liked the sound of her possessive tone. "Now, about the agreement—"

"I'll sign it when we get back," Kate promised, just as Ben finished his sentence.

"—I tore it up."

They both stopped and looked at each other.

"You mean more to me than anything," Ben murmured. "Certainly more than can be measured in dollars and cents. You were right. I never should have let anything like that come between us."

"No. *You* were right," Kate corrected him. "It just took me a while to realize that all the time I was accusing you of not believing in me, I was really trying to hide the fact that I didn't believe in myself." She flashed him a lopsided smile. "Who knows? Maybe it was temporary insanity. But I'm over that now, so you can go ahead and draw up another agreement, because with or without it, I have no intention of ever letting you get away."

His hand came up to stroke her hair. "Sounds to me like it's a moot point."

"Like hell." Kate pretend to glare at him. "I'm trying to compromise here. For Pete's sake, don't muck it up."

"I wouldn't dream of it." Ben eyed the woman who held his future in her hands. "Are you going to argue with me all the way to the altar?"

"Probably." Kate's eyes glinted wickedly. "Although I suppose you could insert a clause about it into that contract of yours."

"You're not going to let that go, are you?"

"Nope." She smiled and held out one hand. "But I'll tell you what. I'll give you the same chance you once gave me—we'll flip for it. Heads, we do it your way. Tails, we do it mine."

"But—"

"No buts." Kate waggled her fingers. "Hand it over."

"If you say so." Ben dug out a dime.

Kate took the coin and flipped it, pausing as she caught it to consider Ben's innocent expression. He was looking entirely too smug not to be up to something. When she lifted her palm, she saw that the coin had come up heads. "I guess you win."

"Not exactly." Ben reached out with the tip of his finger and slowly turned the dime over. Kate's eyes widened as she saw another head appear.

Half outraged, half amused, she tossed him the coin. "I believe," she challenged, "you owe me a raise."

"That's all right." Ben grinned. "You owe me a doughnut."

"Maybe we should call it even."

"Maybe," Ben suggested, "we should call it perfect."

He began to smile and Kate followed his gaze, looking out at the long dark stretch of empty road. "I guess we've come full circle," she said.

"The first of many," Ben murmured, lowering his lips to hers. "Hold on tight, sweet Kate. Here we go again."

PENNY JORDAN

Sins and infidelities . . .
Dreams and obsessions . . .
Shattering secrets
unfold in . . .

THE HIDDEN YEARS

SAGE — stunning, sensual and vibrant, she spent a lifetime distancing herself from a past too painful to confront . . . the mother who seemed to hold her at bay, the father who resented her and the heartache of unfulfilled love. To the world, Sage was independent and invulnerable— but it was a mask she cultivated to hide a desperation she herself couldn't quite understand . . . until an unforeseen turn of events drew her into the discovery of the hidden years, finally allowing Sage to open her heart to a passion denied for so long.

The Hidden Years—a compelling novel of truth and passion that will unlock the heart and soul of every woman.

AVAILABLE IN OCTOBER!
Watch for your opportunity to complete your Penny Jordan set.
POWER PLAY and SILVER will also be available in October.